H. Park Bowden

The Witch of Atlas

a ballooning story

H. Park Bowden

The Witch of Atlas
a ballooning story

ISBN/EAN: 9783337387501

Printed in Europe, USA, Canada, Australia, Japan

Cover: Foto ©Andreas Hilbeck / pixelio.de

More available books at **www.hansebooks.com**

THE
WITCH OF ATLAS

A BALLOONING STORY

BY

H. PARK BOWDEN

> " There she would build herself a windless haven
> Out of the clouds whose moving turrets make
> The bastions of the storm, when through the sky
> The spirits of the tempest thundered by."
>
> *The Witch of Atlas.*—SHELLEY.

LONDON

SAMPSON LOW, MARSTON, SEARLE, & RIVINGTON

Limited

St. Dunstan's House

FETTER LANE, FLEET STREET, E.C.

1889

THE WITCH OF ATLAS.

CHAPTER I.

" Or, when the weary moon was in the wane,
  Or in the noon of interlunar night,
The lady-witch in visions could not chain
  Her spirit; but sailed forth under the light
Of shooting stars."

The Witch of Atlas.

COUNTLESS red lights dotted, in far-ranging parallel lines, the night-darkened face of the deep. They were the beacons of a fishing-fleet, and corresponded in number to that of the boats.

The scenes which they illumined bore a close similarity to each other; tarry decks encumbered with tackle, about which busily moved the uniformly clad figures of the fishermen, generally eight in number. Aboard one vessel, however, the light fell upon a ninth, a tall, erect figure, conspicuous in tweed suit and "deer-stalker."

Weary with poring over musty tomes of law and logic, this individual had turned his back on London to enjoy for a few days the invigorating breezes of Yarmouth; and, determined to imbibe a copious draught of ozone, he had gone out with the fishing-fleet in the company of an old acquaintance, Captain Potter.

His back towards the lamp, this landsman stood idly watching the heaving phosphorescent waters, listening at the same time to the communications of a burly fisherman respecting the winter trawling season, and occasionally making a few comments, or putting a question, in a pleasant tenor voice of refined accent.

Presently the fisherman's duties called him abaft. For a few minutes the other

continued his contemplation of the gleaming surges; then, turning on his heel, he
moved towards the hatchway. The light
now falling full on his face, revealed dark
and noble features of expression not easily
interpreted. The quick, incisive glance
of his dark eyes indicated that astuteness
was prominent among his mental qualities.

With due circumspection, he let himself
down the rickety ladder into the dark
little cabin, the close atmosphere of which
was strongly tainted with fish and tobacco.
Settling himself as comfortably as possible
on a locker at right angles with the grate,
towards whose brightly burning fire he
turned his feet—he closed his eyes, and
fell into a sound sleep. Before long he
was suddenly aroused by a tremendous
noise which grew louder and louder.
Springing to his feet, he mounted the
ladder on to the deck. The cause of
alarm was manifest. A dark, towering
object, bearing one misty light, was

swooping down on the fleet of vessels, that, bereft of sail and mast, were powerless to escape the impending danger.

"Can you make out what it is?" he asked of the skipper, who was hastily binding a quantity of tarred hemps on the end of a pole.

"Swamped if I can!" was the short reply.

"'Pears to me," said a gruff voice near, "like a great hulk toppin' along on her keelson."

"Then Old Nick must be a-steerin' her!" said the skipper, as setting the hemp afire, he raised the flaming mass aloft—a warning already adopted by numbers of the fleet. Far and wide spread the light of the conflagration, disclosing the appalling object to be but a collapsing balloon, whose tiny car just skimmed the face of the deep—a disclosure that caused the terrific uproar to give place to a dead silence.

As the stiff breeze brought it nearer the fleet, the eager watchers perceived that its sole occupant was a woman, and were moved, one and all, to sympathetic excitement. They intently eyed the solitary figure, on which a lamp, hanging from the hoop of the car, shed its hazy rays.

"Starboard yer helm, marm, starboard yer helm!" shouted one of the men.

"I can do nothing to save myself! Do some of you try to catch the ropes, as I drift by," was the appeal carried to them by the wind.

"Aye, aye, ma'am!" was the simultaneous shout of a dozen voices.

On, on swept the looming aërostat.

Suddenly it rose some feet into the air, and the excited smacksmen detected a dark line stretching between the bottom of the car and the heaving sea.

"Ah, the guide-rope," muttered the landsman, hastily pulling off his coat.

As he hurriedly unfastened his boots, he kept a vigilant watch on the advancing balloon with its solitary lamp and passenger. Were both light and life to be extinguished in the dark world of waters?

The landsman being on the outermost smack but one in the second line from the rear, he was in a position to measure the chances of the balloon's capture, which appeared to him very slight; for he saw that its course being in a tangential line, it would come into proximity with one vessel only. His peering eyes could now discern the extreme pallor of the set face which seemed illumined halo-like by the radiance of the hanging lamp.

The balloon approached the critical point—approached and missed it—just beyond the reach of the many hands outstretched towards the loose lengths of rope streaming from the network that enclosed its upper part. A line was flung towards the aëronaut, but it missed her grasp; the vain attempt to seize it all but precipitating her into the sea. Recovering her balance, she caught up a knife, and began desperately severing the ropes connecting the car to the hoop. The gleaming steel had divided three and was at work on a fourth, when a loud splash apprised her of the fact that some one had plunged into the sea.

Through silvery-white tracks and inky-black spaces, that alternately revealed and hid him, the swimmer plied his course towards the aërial waif. The next minute a tremendous swelling cheer broke the hush of suspense. The giant fugitive was captured. But it was evidently as much as its captor could do to impede its course.

" Hold on t'her tail, my baw, I'll tackle her. in a brace o' shakes ! " bawled a strapping fellow on board the smack nearest the point of contest. Foreseeing the emergency, he had been divesting himself of his outer garments and cumbrous boots; and now, having secured around his waist one end of a line, he leapt overboard. His mates ran out the rope according to his headway. A few coils alone remained with them when the seaman reached the struggling landsman. Soon over the water came the shouts, "All right, haul away!" And haul the sailors did full lustily. The two in the water also towing by means of the guide-rope.

More and more towering grew the dark form of the balloon in the eyes of the hauling smacksmen. "Belay there!" said the skipper, when it was drawn within a score of yards of the boat, the car being about on a level with her deck. Then stepping forward to the low bulwark, he touched his hat preliminary to addressing the balloonist, but instead of so doing, he hesitated awkwardly, as though dubious how to accost such a *rara avis*. Finally, raising his hand to his bearded mouth, he abruptly launched his voice.

"Lookee here, marm. I'm fur thinkin' this 'ere boat will be capsizin' bloomin' sharp, if her be rigged with such quar sail as that!"

"No fear of that. The balloon is too far collapsed to work any mischief!" came in impatient tones from one of the swimmers. His peremptory voice was immediately followed by a woman's, clear as a bell. "If you will extinguish that torch, there will be no danger whatever."

At once grasping the overlooked fact, that an explosion was a more impending danger than a capsize, the skipper hastily seized the pole, and thrust its still flaming extremity overboard; a loud hiss, and it was quenched. Then, turning to the men, he bade them haul in. As they obeyed him, their eyes curiously scrutinized the occupant of the wicker-work car.

The next minute the overhanging and

fast collapsing balloon, that had now taken somewhat the form of a parachute, grazed the boat's timbers. While some secured the car and awkwardly assisted the fair aëronaut into the boat, others gave a helping hand to her rescuers. One of the rescuers, picking up his garments from where he had hastily thrown them, disappeared below, while the other aided the men, who, in compliance with the lady's request, were overhauling the balloon into a position that would allow of the removal of the indiarubber band from the valve, and the consequent free escape of the remaining gas. The band having been removed, the lady fell back a few paces from the eager knot of smacksmen.

Thrusting back his dripping hair, her deliverer, the landsman, moved to join her, where she stood by the extemporized lamp-post.

The lady's small, finely-cut features, instinct with subdued excitement, deeply

impressed him. As he met her eyes,
deep

<blockquote>
' As are
Two openings of unfathomable night
Seen through a tempest's cloven roof,"
</blockquote>

they seemed to flash light on his memory,
revealing a reflection of the past. Once,
when wearied with a day's exploration of
Mount Atlas' heights and recesses, he
had laid him down to rest, as dewy purple
nightfall approached, on a fragrant grassy
bed, canopied by butting rock. Again, in
imagination, he drowsily watched a pearly
crescent rise above the silvered outline of
the opposite mountain, darkened with many
a dusky cypress. It was just, seemingly,
poised on its nether tip, when a black-
robed figure passed, with swift and noise-
less footstep, the observer's shadowed
resting-nook. The level moonbeams
showed the watcher a face of gleaming
fairness, lit by forward-gazing eyes of
sombre splendour. The watcher's spell-

bound eyes followed the fair figure, until a jutting rock hid her from his view. Springing to his feet he hastened to the rocky angle and looked eagerly down a shadowy winding vale, tracked with moonlight, but saw no dark-robed figure. Thus baffled he returned to his lowly couch, and remembered how

> "A lady-witch there lived on Atlas' mountain,
> Within a cavern by a secret fountain,"

and deciding, to his fancy's satisfaction, that he had seen no other than that lady-witch, he fell asleep, to dream she re-appeared on the opposite mountain-ridge, and, with sudden prank, set the crescent spinning on its point.

Since that night, seven times sevenfold,

> "The mother of the months had bent
> Her bow beside the folding-star;"

and now behold, the wizard lady stood before him, encompassing his whole being with

> "The magic circle of her voice and eyes."

"How can I ever thank you! But for your prompt kindness and exertion, I should certainly have lost my balloon, and probably my life."

With an effort he recalled himself from his abstraction to attend to her clear flowing voice, and, in a vague perplexity, taking her extended hand, he expressed his happiness in having been of service to her.

"I am afraid I and my poor *Serena* are greatly in the way," she said, glancing towards the amorphous balloon, now emitting its gas over the boat's side. "I shall be glad when I can pack her into the car; I would I could make myself of smaller compass."

"Dwindle away into one of your boots comparatively speaking," he said, with cursory pleasantry, adding seriously, "I greatly regret that we cannot offer you better accommodation. There is some sort of a cabin below—but, I forget I have changed boats !　Though, doubtless, there is just such another little cabin and bright fire aboard this one.　Yes, I see there is," he added, glancing down the cramped hatchway near which they stood.

" I am very glad of that, for your sake," she said.　"You must feel wretched in those wet clothes."

" It may be there is some spare gear on board that I could don whilst my own is drying," he said.

" Do go then at once and inquire," she urged.

Gratified at her concern on his behalf, he made for the skipper.　In a minute he returned to her, having ascertained that there were a few things stowed away in a locker below, belonging to that worthy, who was now gone to rummage for them. He stubbornly delayed following him, until he had placed a fish-crate in the least exposed quarter of the deck, and covered it with a rug he fetched from the car.

Having cast a glance aft, and satisfied herself that the men were adhering to their promise, that a lighted pipe should not come near the balloon, the smack's fair visitant fell to watching the pearly bloom that came and went on the herring-teeming water.

Presently, on looking round she found her late companion had rejoined her, now attired in rough blue guernsey, wide canvas trousers, and big sou'-wester, whose aft-brim made an incongruous background to his aristocratic features.

" Mr. Peggotty, at your service," he said, touching the curtailed forebrim of his sou'-wester, " alias," he continued, bowing, " Derrick O'Rorke."

" A name I shall ever remember with gratitude," she said earnestly, then added simply, " Mine is Gytha Keppel."

" I am afraid, Miss Keppel, you must find this rolling very disagreeable, after the smooth sailing of your aërial vessel."

"Nevertheless, I am thankful to have made the exchange. I suppose these are fishing-boats?"

"Yes, the herring-fleet; this is a Yarmouth boat."

"What a number of lights there are!" she said, casting a glance along the far-stretching lines of beacons. "When, on descending below the clouds, I first saw them, I took them for street-lamps."

"I can fancy they had that effect," he said, his glance following hers. "It must have shocked you when you discovered your mistake!" he added, turning his eyes on her pale face.

"It did indeed, Mr. O'Rorke; but, seeing so many boats, I took heart again. What an uproar the men did make!"

"Yes, but considering the thousands of strong lungs that raised it, it is not surprising that it was somewhat deafening," he said, smiling.

" Thousands ! " she repeated, in an astonished tone.

" You must understand that when the rear boats saw you and raised the alarm, it was taken up by the fore ranks. They took your balloon for some ship bearing down on them, and were apprehensive lest any of the boats should be swamped. They are all in a crippled condition you see," he said explanatorily.

" Yes, when I saw that, and found myself drifting out to sea, I decided to cut the ropes and take my chance in the car, it is provided with a cork keel."

" So I observed, and it struck me as an excellent precaution."

" You must wonder at my choosing such a strange hour for an ascent. But I only intended it to be a captive one, such as I had made several times with some of our friends last night, when Mrs. Colborne, my aunt, held a reception."

" Captive ascents, how charming ! "

he exclaimed, on the impulse of a wish that it had been his good fortune to make one of the guests. " Instead of relaxing oneself on the stair of oak, or some such wood, as one is so often glad to do now to escape crowded reception-rooms; how much more pleasant to

> " Ascend the stair of some star-beam rare,"

and

> " Hear the roll
> Of the mighty spheric chime."

He could see a smile flickering about her lips as she made answer,—

" But the star-beams being particularly rare, we ascended instead on the beams of a Bengal light ; and we only heard the ' roll ' made by the musicians below."

" Nevertheless it must have been most delightful. How many will your balloon raise ? "

" Not more than two when loaded with ballast, grapnel, and such like; but, not requiring these, we were able to ascend in quartettes, except in one case, when a ponderous old gentleman rose with his daughter and myself."

"I envy that ponderous old gentleman."

" Your envy is misplaced. He was woefully uneasy lest the rope connecting us with the earth should break, or the balloon explode or the car give way. He vowed on landing he would never rise to heaven again, at least, in the flesh."

O'Rorke laughed, he had not looked for drollery from this sombre-eyed witch.

" And so you were minded to make an ascent alone."

" Yes, when our guests had departed I felt too restless to think of sleep, and resolved to flee into the clouds to exercise the unquiet spirit possessing me."

" Ah, what hour was that ?" he asked, wondering whether the restlessness that had caused her to seek solitude, arose from happy excitement or troubled disturbance.

"It must have been about three o'clock when I left Chelsea. I had been up not more than half an hour, and was about to descend by means of the windlass, when the *Serena* suddenly shot up. At first I thought the rope must have given way, but I soon remembered how eager Shootoo, a monkey my father made a pet of, had been to accompany me, and how angrily he had howled when Thrupp—the man who takes charge of the *Serena*— drove him off. I feel sure that he must have cut the rope out of revenge."

"The imp! He deserves to be hanged therewith! How it must have dismayed you to find yourself at the mercy of the winds."

"I confess it did, when I found it was impossible to get at the valve-rope. Thrupp had loosely knotted it up out of reach of any curious fingers. I could only hope for a condensation, but that hope turned to fear when I remembered I had no ballast, wherewith to moderate my descent, should the condensation be great. I was glad to find the instrument case was in its place under the seat, and I had the key in my pocket, having changed my evening dress for this that I usually wear on my aërial travels. I could not unpack the compass fast enough. It told me I was drifting towards the north, while the barometer showed my altitude to be over 1,900 feet."

" How anxiously you must have watched those instruments ! "

"I did little else. They indicated, though, but little variation in my course, until an hour and thirty minutes had passed, when the barometer told me the *Serena* was decreasing her altitude; and soon after the needle pointed out that she had sunk into a current that would bear her out to sea. How I wished for rain, that it might hasten the depression in time for her to save the land. There were clouds beneath me, so I could see no lights, but I distinctly heard the note of a mole-cricket."

"A sound I have always had a great dislike to, but its sharp pitch must have been welcome to your ears!" he said, drawing a mental picture of her, speeding in her aërial chariot through black space.

"Much more so, I can assure you, than that which followed, a sound as of breakers, followed by a rapid condensation of gas, which convinced me I must be over the sea. But when I sunk below the clouds and saw these beacons, I thought I must have been mistaken, and was descending near a town. Indeed, mindful of chimneys, I was beginning to wind up the guide-rope, when I saw the lights came from lines of boats, and not from streets. I shall never forget the minutes when it was doubtful whether the current would sweep me past them, away into that hopeless blackness!" looking over the waters to where no beacon shed its ray, or herring-shoal its soft shimmer.

"How anxious your friends must be feeling about you!"

"I daresay they know nothing about what has happened as yet, for I told my maid and Thrupp not to wait up for me. But I must telegraph to my aunt directly we reach Yarmouth. Ah, now I can pack the *Serena!*" she exclaimed, rising.

Turning his head, he saw a dark mass lying on the deck, and springing up from his seat—an empty cask—he said,—

"It does seem practicable now to dispose of her as you desired. Will you entrust the disposal to me? I assure you I will be carefulness itself."

"I should be most glad if you would help me. I suppose the men will begin to haul in their nets presently; I see the day is breaking," she said, glancing towards the faint line of light defining the horizon.

" Pray don't you trouble, Miss Keppel, the deck is quite slippery. If I need assistance, I will get one of the men to help me."

Whilst Derrick O'Rorke was busy aft, she watched the grey line broaden into a luminous zone. Soon the wide stretch of tumbling sea was plainly visible, no longer mysterious with jetty blackness or alluring with fitful gleams of soft radiance.

So, the wind blowing freshly against one pale cheek, she sat and watched.

> " And withal did ever keep
> The tenour of her contemplations calm,
> With open eyes, closed feet, and folded palm."

CHAPTER II.

" With rapid race
The light sail coyly flies the wind's embrace,
Eager to be pursued the while."

W. J. A.

By the time O'Rorke had reduced this cumbersome tissue to a compactly folded bale, and stowed it away in the car, the deck was a scene of busy commotion, attendant on the hauling in of the net.

"We shall soon set sail now," said O'Rorke, returning to the figure sitting on the rug-covered crate.

"What an overwhelming draught!" she said, watching the interminable meshy length, as straining under the weight of the night's harvest, it was drawn, all gleaming and dripping, from the sea.

"I am afraid you will have every reason to ' gather in ' your ' braw peliss,' " he said, looking down on her mouse-coloured dress.

"I shall never hear that song again but I shall see this scene ; " and it was a thoughtful look that she turned on the busy fleet, each boat of which was so exact a counterpart of her neighbour.

There was that in her remark which jarred on his contented mood. It was a suggestive remark. And he was averse to thinking of the present as lapsed into the past, of this now existing companionship dissolved into a remembrance only. Taking advantage of her averted eyes, he scrutinized her features, now illumined by the dawn. But already had those features become minutely imprinted on his mind, even to the little black mole, marking the white curve of her chin.

And now the net was safely boarded; the take proving a highly satisfactory one, inasmuch that even the skipper's grim visage relaxed. Moreover, he agreeably received O'Rorke's request, that he would be good enough to run the boat alongside number 229, the *Mary Jane*, in order that he might recover his coat, &c.

The men working with a will, the mast was soon re-erected, the sail set, and the vessel tacking for number 229, which boat was not as yet under way.

As the smack was in the act of running by number 229, a dark bundle was thrown by one of the latter's crew on to the deck of the former, towards which were also directed sundry glances of open curiosity, which at once singled out that favoured boat's fair passenger.

Possessing himself of the said bundle, O'Rorke went below. As the last of the wan yellow beacons disappeared, the sun's strong red disk shot its broad level beams over the line of water, revealing the glancing whiteness of the sails that were now every moment being set.

"By the powers, one might take it for a regatta!" was the remark that caused Gytha Keppel to turn her head, and for the first time she beheld O'Rorke "in his habit as he lived," neither shrinking in drenched clothes, nor travestying in borrowed ones.

"Yes, it is quite exciting to watch them, they all seem so eager to be foremost!" she responded, as together they observed the gay company of vessels swiftly pursuing their course; "I had no idea they could look so graceful. And how quickly they unfolded their wings, and took flight! I wish a balloon were as quickly inflated as a vessel is rigged."

"You think of returning to Chelsea by aërial route," he said, with a quick, questioning look.

"Now that the wind has so favourably

changed, I feel tempted to do so. Of course, there are gas-works at Yarmouth ? "

"Yes, and conveniently accessible. I hope you will consider me at your service, and allow me to undertake the little matter of getting the *Serena* conveyed there," he said, with eager courtesy.

" Thank you very much, Mr. O'Rorke ; your kind offer decides me. I have a great dislike to railway travelling."

" I can imagine you must find it insufferably irksome, after experiencing your delightful mode of travelling. You must be thoroughly conversant with the science to venture on an excursion alone. I presume you have made many ascents."

" The last was my forty-ninth."

" Indeed ! You must have pretty well made ' the grand tour of the skies.' "

A smile lit up her face, then quickly died away.

"Ballooning was my father's favourite recreation," she replied, in a subdued tone; "and from the time I was twelve years old, he often used to take me with him in his ascents. He only objected to my joining him in those he made from Algiers."

"Algiers!" he repeated quickly.

"Yes, we always wintered there, on account of his health. The only one I have ever spent elsewhere was the one following his death, three years ago."

She paused, and, seeing that her feelings were painfully moved, he for a while turned his eyes on a smack running near, and preserved a sympathetic silence. Presently, he broke it by a question he hoped would beguile her into speaking of her Algerian life.

"You have, then, never ascended from the Dark Continent?"

"Only captive ascents, on account of

the sea being so near, and the inland so wild. But captive though they be, they are very enjoyable when the atmosphere is clear, and the Mediterranean can be seen stretching away on one side, and Mount Atlas on the other."

To his ears the latter name fell from her lips like a spell.

"It must be glorious! Climb and toil how he would, an earthling could never reap such a bounteous eye-harvest as you must, in the scythe-sweep of a glance. Does your foot ever go gleaning, after your eye has done its reaping? I mean among the fair vales of those mountains."

"Yes, it is very prone to do so," she replied, her face taking an expression that told him how sweet were her memories

."Of the white stream, and of the forest green."

"To speak literally of reaping," she

went on slowly, " Mrs. Meredith, the lady who lives with me, and I often go there and watch the reapers; and sometimes we climb the mountain to see how the vines are flourishing. My father possessed several vineyards on one of the Tell mountains, in which he used to take a great interest, so I still retain them. He had a log-cabin built up there, where we rest after our climb of nearly 2000 feet."

" I remember admiring the condition of some vineyards thereabouts," said O'Rorke, resolving to broach the theme of his thoughts.

" You have been on the Atlas, then ! "

" Yes, I passed a day there about four years since, climbing and exploring, until I could climb and explore no more for very fatigue, so threw myself down to rest. When, 'It might have been a fancy, or it might have been a dream,' but as I lay there, the very counterpart of yourself passed quickly by my nook."

· " About four years since ? " she repeated, with a questioning glance that ended in a look of sad comprehension. " Was it, do you remember, the evening of the 13th of November ? "

" The selfsame ! "

" Doubtless then it was I. We, my father and I, had been up on the mountain, and as we were descending he caught his foot in the trunk of a tree, and was thrown forward with such force that he dislocated his knee."

" How unfortunate! And you were going for assistance when I saw you ? "

" Yes, I was on my way to a vine-dresser's cottage."

" How I wish I had known, that I might have gone in your stead! I hope the accident was not serious? But, of course, a dislocated knee *is* serious."

" It was, indeed! He never walked after without the use of a crutch." Her voice drooped sadly into silence.

In the course of their ensuing conversation, he intimated to her that he was
studying for the law, and intended on the
morrow to bring his few days' sojourn in
Yarmouth to a close, and return to the
legal atmosphere—which atmosphere, he
might say, he had inhaled with the first
breath he had drawn, having béen born in
the Inner Temple. Then, in answer to a
question of hers, he went on to say that,
his father having successfully conducted
numerous law-suits, and made himself
of high repute, had entered into a suit
of a more sentimental nature, with
a ward in chancery—the niece and dis-
puted heiress of General Boswell—the
suit at last satisfactorily terminating in
the lady, and the Court, granting their
long-withheld sanction to the union. As
was then not at all an unusual proceeding with Inns-of-Court benedicts, he had
installed his wife in his chambers in the
Inner Temple, where ultimately he, their

only son, first saw the light; and in that legal sanctuary had passed his tender years, a law-consecrated child Derrick.

"The first joyous emotion of which I have any recollection," he said, in a slower tone, "was occasioned by my mother equipping me with reins of red tape; and my first grievous one, by my father chastising me for making a paper-ship of an important document, and all but reducing it to pulp in one of the fountains."

"That was a crime indeed!" she said, a smiling light in her attentive eyes, that filled with sympathetic interest as he proceeded to say, how, on waking one morning, his nurse imparted the—to his childish mind—ambiguous information that he was an orphan.

The previous evening, while returning from Twickenham, a fatal accident had befallen his parents, their boat being run down by a pleasure-steamer. Within a week of the calamity, miles of

English land and Irish sea lay between him and his birthplace; his father's brother having received him and his baby sister into his family. When he again entered the Temple, he had more than quadruplicated his years, and, having now been keeping terms for three years, expected shortly to be called to the Bar.

Yarmouth was now well in sight; the green foliage of the trees, and red roofs of the houses, showing with fine effect between the thickly-standing masts. In a few minutes they passed between the old wooden piers, flanking the mouth of the Yare.

As they slowly proceeded up the river, the bold looks of curiosity wherewith those on the busy wharf eyed his companion, caused O'Rorke's brows to contract unpleasantly. His face turned white, and hers crimson, as a leering loafer bawled after the smack,—

"Hallo, skipper! Be her a mermaid ye've hawled in? Do her end in a tail?"

Audible amusement, both ashore and aboard, followed this coarse sally.

"The knave—the clowns!" muttered O'Rorke. "Shall we go down into the cabin until the boat is moored?" he said, turning to her. "It is an uninviting hole, but—"

"It will be better than being here," she said, with an asperity that told of keen annoyance.

"What a queer, dark little place," she said a minute later, as with fading colour and clearing brow, she seated herself on a locker.

"It has not even a fire to improve its aspect now," he remarked, looking down on the dead ashes in the rusty grate; "and now, Miss Keppel," he went on, leaning his elbow on a convenient rung of the ladder, and regarding her with a business-like air, "you must be sadly in want of a cup of tea. There is an excellent hotel on the Parade. Will you allow me to conduct you—"

"Thank you very much, Mr. O'Rorke, but I dislike the thought of going to an hotel," she said hastily, adding in a moderated tone, "I daresay I can find a confectioner's in the town."

He looked at her dubiously, as though he did not at all fancy the notion, but could not improve on it.

After a minute's pondering, he said eagerly,—

"An idea has just struck me! The skipper of the boat in which I started—a regular Yarmouth bloater, with a Devonshire dumpling of a wife—owns a domicile in a certain Row close by, where I am sure you would find welcome and cheer of sterling, if homely, quality; that is to say, if my idea recommends itself to you."

A needless addition, seeing the look of relief with which she had received it.

" I should be most glad to adopt it, if you feel confident they would excuse the intrusion, and be willing to accommodate me ? "

" As ' willin' ' as Barkiss, I assure you. ' Excuse the intrusion ! ' They will value it as a visit of honour. Then, before I see about getting a vehicle for the balloon, I will conduct you thither."

" But my telegram—I must see to that first," she said.

" You must allow me to dispatch that, on my way to the works."

" I think the boat has come to a stand-still. I will run up and see," and he disappeared up the ladder.

She had but time to scribble down her aunt's address when his figure again darkened the opening.

" Yes, Miss Keppel, they are mooring her on," he said, bending and looking down.

So, quickly rising, she mounted the ladder, accepting the help of the hand he stretched down.

The deck was already in the stir of unloading. As she passed the skipper, she shook hands with him, by way of leave-taking, and tendered him her "fare," as she called it; her manner expressing a sense of obligation—nothing more. But it also expressed a deep sense of gratitude, when, coming again to a halt, she thanked her other preserver, concluding with, " Will you please accept, and turn this into tobacco ?" and O'Rorke saw a golden coin exchange the fair softness of her hand for the brown horniness of the smacksman's.

Leaving the vessel, they plunged into the midst of the jostling crowd, and confusing hubbub of shrill female and gruff male voices, over which a vigorously rung bell maintained a brassy triumph.

Between numbers of carts, piles of fish-crates, and eager knots of fish-fags, O'Rorke adroitly piloted his fair charge. Presently they turned off from the wharf, into a Row so narrow, that, finding it a difficult matter to walk abreast, O'Rorke soon dropped a pace behind, their conversation being thus rendered doubly charming to his mind by an occasional profile-revealing turn of the hooded head in advance of him. Moreover, he could observe how light and easily she stepped along over the rough, ankle-twisting coble-stones. How some of his fair acquaintances would have limped, hobbled, and halted, over these selfsame touchstones of grace!

Emerging from this narrow passage, they crossed a main street, and entered another Row of wider dimensions. As, side by side, they continued on their way, O'Rorke advanced a request that had been near his lips for some time past, namely, that she would allow him to accompany her in her ascent. She had probably been anticipating this request, and had secretly resolved to grant it. Being such an experienced balloonist, she counted the request of but little more importance than if her new acquaintance, to whom she was so deeply indebted, had asked to accompany her in the same railway carriage to London. She therefore granted the favour without demur, much to O'Rorke's gratification.

CHAPTER III.

" Oh thou, who ; plumed with strong desire,
Would float above the earth, beware ! "
Shelley.

" This is the house, Miss Keppel," he
announced, as they reached an open doorway, overhung by a projecting upper
window; " and here is Mrs. Potter," he
added, lifting his hat, as from the dark
interior there appeared a middle-aged
woman, chiefly remarkable for plump
rotundity of face and figure.

" Good-day to 'ee, sir," she said, dropping
a courtesy. " I was thinkin' to myself that
p'r'aps 'ee'd come along wi' Joe. But I
reckoned wrong I see," and she looked
with sharp wonder towards Gytha.

O'Rorke hastened to acquaint her with

the circumstances that had brought a would-be guest to her door.

With a fluster of hospitality, she begged the lady would come in and make the best of things. " But bain't 'ee comin' in, sir," she broke off, seeing that he remained on the threshold.

" I will partake of your hospitality with pleasure, Mrs. Potter, after attending to a little business at the gas-works. Now, Miss Keppel, what shall I say to your aunt?"

" Say, please, 'No cause for alarm. Safe at Yarmouth. Am returning to-day.' You have the address?"

" Yes; 'Mrs. Colbourne, Rutland Lodge, Chelsea.' I will return as quickly as possible; but pray don't wait breakfast, Miss Keppel. *Au revoir.*"

" Sure, but 'tis a pity Mr. O'Rorke is obliged to leave 'ee, Miss," lamented the housewife, as she conducted her visitor up a steep flight of stairs, " I am 'fraid 'ee will find it lonesome like; but I s'pose 'a couldn't put off his business at the works."

"It is to see about the filling of my balloon," said Gytha. "I hope they will be able to spare me the gas."

"La, now! be them there things filled with gas! I always thought them was filled with air. However do 'ee live in that nasty stuff, miss? I've heard as how 'tis sure to kill 'ee, if 'ee are shut up in it."

"But I am not shut up in it," said Gytha, quickly guessing the woman was labouring under the mistake common with simple folks, that aëronauts travel *inside* their balloons; "there is a car attached to the balloon, and unless the gas is escaping very freely from the neck it does not affect the air I breathe."

"Now only to think! I never heard tell of no car before. But bain't 'ee 'fraid of tumblin' out?"

"Oh, no; the car is as steady as this room." They were now standing in what was evidently the state-room of the house. "Now, miss," said Mrs. Potter, throwing open another door, which gave admittance to an adjoining bedroom, " I'm sure 'ee·will be glad of a wash. And I'll go down and hurry with the breakfast."

In a few minutes, having removed her hood and jacket, Gytha returned to the sitting-room, and seated herself in the projecting window.

Her eyes, having studied the herring-bone masonry of the opposite house until they were weary, turned to the quaintly furnished sitting-room. What an irregular room it was ! The floor and ceiling forming a decided incline towards the window, and the walls deviating from a straight line, insomuch that the further end of the room was but one-third the breadth of the other. A low, chintz-covered sofa just fitted into the contracted space ; a cosy nook, reached only by sidling along a ponderous table, whose broad round face shone right bravely despite the ravages of time ; indeed, the only thing that did not appear age-worn, was a handsomely framed portrait which hung above the carved chimney-piece, a portrait that Gytha regarded with an attention that showed the fair pictured face had deeply engaged her interest—as well it might, seen amidst such incongruous surroundings. Its dainty grace would have attracted attention had it been hung in a gallery of "fair women." The term "woman," however, was scarcely applicable to it. A girlish blitheness looked saucily from the black-fringed blue eyes, bloomed softly on the dimpled cheek, smiled archly on the crimson-warm lips.

Leaning her head against the high back of her roomy basket-chair, Gytha studied each charming detail of the perfect whole, until her eyelids, oppressed with drowsiness, drooped into repose.

Ten minutes later they started into

wakefulness, at the sound of a turning handle and clinking china.

"La! now, if I hav'n't agone and wakened 'ee!" exclaimed Mrs. Potter, halting in the doorway that seemed scarcely wide enough to admit the enormous, well-laden tray she carried.

"I suppose I must have been asleep, for I was certainly dreaming," said Gytha, as she rose and placed a chair *vis-à-vis* with a fellow; a performance Mrs. Potter's right foot had been making dislocating attempts to effect.

"Thank 'ee, miss; but 'ee shouldn't have troubled," she said, depositing her tray on the makeshift stand. "I'm glad 'ee had a nap, miss; maybe it's a bit rested 'ee feel?" she said, spreading a blue-white cloth over the table's broad face.

"Thank you, I did not feel tired, or sleepy, to my knowledge; but while I was looking at that portrait, I drifted into dreaming of it."

" Bain't shea booty ! " said her hostess, enthusiasm in her tone, and pride in her eyes. " I daresay 'ee wonder how I came by such a picter as that, and maybe 'ee would like to know ? Well, 'twas just this," she went on, proceeding to arrange on the table the huddled contents of the tray; " Joe, that's my old man, saved that very young lady from drownin'. She was a-bathin' one mornin' and ventured too far, as young ladies will. Her father, Mr. O'Rorke, was that grateful 'a would have done anything for Joe ; and Miss Eileen she used to come here often to see 'un, and afore she went back to Ireland she got quite fond of 'un like, and me too for the matter o' that. And 'ee may be sure such a sweet young lady found a place in our hearts ; I cried like a babby the day she went away, and so did Joe, though 'a wouldn't own to it. Well, would 'ee b'lieve it, nigh on a month after she left, there was a gran' knockin' at the door, and when I ran out, there stood a carrier-man with a great case that filled up the door-way. I told 'un it couldn't be for here nohow, but 'a said, ' Bain't your husban's name, Cap'n Potter ? ' ' Ess sure,' I said, ' Well, then, this here case is for he, and none other,' 'a said, and carried it straight into the kitchen. When my old man came home, 'a knocked off the cover o' the box, and there was that bootiful picter ! And as like to her it is as two peas. Then us found a dear little letter tucked in at the back, sayin' as how she'd had it painted for Joe and me. The next summer, two years agone now, they came again, and Miss Eileen brought her cousin to see me. But bless me, if I don't look sharp 'a will be back again afore I've got the breakfast up ! And there's, I might 'a bin cuttin' the bread and butter while I've bin pratin'," she said, grasping the loaf with one hand and the bread-knife in the other.

" Pray let me do that, Mrs. Potter,"
said Gytha, going to the table.

" 'Deed, miss, I should be real glad
if 'ee would, for I left the frying-pan
on the hob, and its burnin' the fish
maybe if I don't look after 'em," and
she· hastened downstairs to prevent that
disaster.

The sound of her footsteps had scarcely
died away, when the stairs again creaked
under ascending footfalls; but instead of
Mrs. Potter, O'Rorke appeared in the
doorway.

Certes, there was little that was weird
and much that was homely about the
witch of the present, was the thought
that passed through his mind, as his
glance alighted on the lithesome figure
bending over the breakfast-table, at once
noting how dark was the hair coiled
around the shapely head, and how fair the
sweeping neck.

" This is a speedier return than I

anticipated," she said, as turning her head she revealed to him a faintly flushing cheek.

"A trolly was quickly forthcoming," he said, with an easy smile, "and we made all despatch in getting to the works, where I left the *Serena* gradually recovering from her exhaustion."

"I have been wondering whether you would think of the suspending ropes I cut. I intended to ask you to get them replaced," she said, glancing at him questioningly.

"Yes, I have seen to that, and also to the ballast-bags. I think I have been singularly fortunate this morning, having in each instance found the right man in the right place."

Mrs. Potter now hurried in with the replenished tray, and quickly added to the table a brightly shining teapot, a dish of fried herrings, and some boiled eggs. She then placed a chair for Gytha, who was about to take it, when she observed that the table was laid for two only.

"I hope you are going to join us, Mrs. Potter," she said, turning to that good dame.

"'Deed, miss, but I broke my fast hours agone. But if so be 'ee would like, I will sit me down and do a bit o' knittin'," and having placed a second chair for O'Rorke, she moved to the window, and taking from her apron-pocket a legless stocking, she disposed of her own ample person in the roomy basket-chair.

"They were willing to supply the gas, then," said Gytha, handing him a most capacious cup of tea.

"Yes, quite so. Indeed, the director evinced great interest in the *Serena*. How long does the inflating process generally take?"

"About two hours."

"Then we shall be able to start before noon," he said, carefully dissecting his fish.

Not receiving any reply, he looked up quickly, to perceive an expression on her face that rather puzzled him.

"I wish you were not so desirous of making the ascent," she said, in a concerned tone; "accidents are liable to happen, and I should feel responsible for your safety," she concluded, with a smile.

"If," said he, "there is no weighty objection in my avoirdupois, there can be no likelihood of my causing a disaster. I hope in the case of a common casualty to be of service to you. Do you know Mrs. Potter," he went on, glancing at the industrious knitter, "that I am about to take a peep into cloudland?"

"Awh, 'ee bain't agoin' up in the balloon surely, sir?" she asked, looking up with dolorous surprise.

"Yes," he nodded gaily. "'All are not born to soar,' but assuredly I was!"

"Maybe 'ee will soar down'ards when 'ee will least fancy," she said, her doleful tone changing to an emphatic one. "Drat them old belloons, I say! Excoose me, miss, but it do' seem so tempting providence to try to go up so high. I've been wonderin' to myself if 'twould be of any good for me to try to turn 'ee from goin' up again yourself."

"It is very good of you, Mrs. Potter, to trouble about me; but it would be the greatest deprivation to me to give up my recreation."

"Well, I do hope 'ee will be careful. How high up do 'ee go, miss?"

"Between six and eight thousand feet generally, but I have been carried as high as four miles."

"Bless my life! I should be 'fraid of goin' right up through the sky!"

"Oh, there is no fear of that," asserted the aëronaut, confining her amusement—augmented by the glance that O'Rorke, directed towards her—to a quivering smile.

"I am glad to hear that," said O'Rorke, with an assumed air of relief. "It would be an awkward intrusion. We should be literally what the Polynesians term foreigners, pápalangi, or in our language, heaven-bursters."

"There's Joe!" exclaimed Mrs. Potter, starting up, as a gruff throat-clearing sound rose from below. Telling them to bump on the floor if they needed anything, she hastened down to welcome the returned night-toiler.

A silence fell on the two she had left that was at length broken by O'Rorke observing,—

"It is unfortunate the day has become so overcast; but I assume it does not much signify so long as the wind keeps in the right quarter. I do hope it may not shift round to the west. I suppose you find the temperature vary greatly during an ascent?"

"Yes, indeed; it seems at times as though the months were running riot in space. Sometimes I encounter a soft shower, that makes me fancy April is hovering near. Then I suddenly find myself enwrapped in a fog such as November brings to the earth; to presently mount into the heat of August. And, again, I have left summer holding terrestrial reign, and risen into a snow-storm."

"Then doubtless you have encountered a thunder-storm?" he said, remembering how the wind-riding witch, "laughed to hear the fire-balls roar behind."

"Yes, on two occasions," she replied. "The first time I was with my father, and we surmounted the storm and watched it from above."

"It must have been a grand spectacle. I once viewed one from the Alps; but your experience must have been an improvement on mine."

At this minute Mrs. Potter re-entered the room. With a formal, embarrassed air, she addressed her fair guest,—

"My husban', miss, 'a have sent me

to tell 'ee 'a would be main glad to see
the last of 'ee, if so be 'ee will be good
enough to let 'im be alongside when the
belloon goes up?"

"Certainly, Mrs. Potter," she answered,
with a relieved readiness that interpreted
to O'Rorke her startled look at the opening of the good dame's speech. His eyes
fell, and he made use of his handkerchief.
"I was intending to ask you if you would
accompany me to the works," continued
Miss Keppel. "Will you tell your husband we hope to ascend about noon?"

"Thank 'ee kindly, miss, 'twill be a rare
sight for us. Joe be that curious to see
how her be rigged: 'a will be up to offer
'ee his dooty, miss, as soon as ever 'a have
had bit and sop."

"I shall be pleased to make his acquaintance," she said, rising from the
table.

As O'Rorke also rose, his eyes met the

lifelike gaze of the fair semblance above the chimney-piece. Immediately averting them, he passed on to the window.

"What a splendid chrysanthemum!" he said, regarding with genuine admiration the mass of fanciful green leaves and creamy-white blooms, adorning the open casement. "Will you spare me one for my button-hole, Mrs. Potter?"

"Ess sure, sir, as many as ever 'ee like," she said, and hastening over she snipped off flower after flower, heedless of protestation.

"There, sir, I'm proud 'ee should fancy 'em. Maybe 'ee would like a few, miss?"

"Surely there is plenty for both here," said O'Rorke, looking down on his gigantic "buttonhole," and extracting therefrom a single flower, he tendered the rest to Gytha, who inserted the sweet-smelling bunch in her waistband.

"Faith, if she be not a witch, she is

decidedly an enigma! Who would imagine, seeing her just now engaged in her domestic task, and talking so sociably the while, that she could ever find pleasure in welkin exile. Fancy Eileen voluntarily plunging into darkness and solitude! 'What differs more than man from man?' asked the Bard of Rydal. What differs more than maid from maid? ask I!"

So queried to himself the "Knight Templar"—such he had been dubbed by his Dublin kith and kin—as he retraced his way to the gas-works; Gytha having arranged to follow shortly with Mrs. Potter.

CHAPTER IV.

"Thou serenest air,
Through which the sun walks burning without beams!
And ye swift whirlwinds, who on poised wings
Hung mute and moveless o'er yon hushed abyss."
Shelley.

" La! miss, there be silk enough to make a dozen gowns!"

This exclamation, so decidedly fraught with envy, broke from Mrs. Potter, who had twice silently circumambulated the reviving balloon, the first time in gaping astonishment, the second time engaged in a calculation that reduced the alternate white and crimson gores to thirty-six in number.

" Yes, it must have cost a considerable sum to clothe such a giantess 'in silk attire,' " rejoined O'Rorke, gazing up at the towering spheroid, that was gently rocking to and fro, as if unable to passively suffer her restraint.

" A dozen gowns, if it would make one," regretfully repeated Mrs. Potter.

" I b'lieve ye'r haukering fur to strip her ! " said the skipper, looking round, with a broad grin to see the effect of his jocular accusation on the gasmen standing by.

" Don't *'ee* bark ! " retorted his wife. " Who was it as said jist this minute, as how there was rope enough about her to rig a ship ? "

A general laugh applauded her sharp reply.

" But wherever be the car, miss ? " she asked, looking round. " Be thiky thing, it ? " moving towards the spot where stood a wicker-work structure, six feet in length and four in breadth. " It do look cosy," she commented, leaning over the side, smoothing the crimson velvet covering the well-padded benches fixed at either end, and bestowing an admiring glance on the bear's-skin rug that had been replaced. "Whatever fur do 'ee want that, miss?" she questioned, indicating the machinery that occupied the centre of the car.

"That is the windlass, for raising and lowering the guide-rope," explained Gytha. "And now, Mrs. Potter, will you come in with me and sit down while I unpack the instruments?" she added, touching what appeared an ornamental piece of wood affixed without one side of the car, but which, to Mrs. Potter's surprise, magically unfolded into steps. On account of their frail appearance, it needed some persuasion to induce her to avail herself of this means of entry. At last she was comfortably seated, and watched the aëronaut with lively interest, who, drawing a small case from beneath one of the benches, proceeded to unpack from between layers of wadding, various instruments, explaining the use of each before she attached it to a board projecting beyond one side of the carriage. The skipper, who had hove-to alongside, giving an attentive ear and eye, as hygrometer, thermometer, chronometer, and barometers, aneroid and mercurial, were severally introduced. This, to her, somewhat dry source of interest, being exhausted, Mrs. Potter again turned her attention to the oscillating *Serena.*

"Doth she wobble like that when she be up, miss?" she asked.

"Oh, no! At least not unless she loses an undue quantity of gas or ballast," Gytha quickly replied, regarding the now shapely balloon with pardonable pride.

"I 'spects yer find more nor a capful o' wind when yer gets well up, miss," said the fisherman.

"On the contrary, I never feel a breath," she replied, to his blank astonishment.

"In one of my ascents a most violent hurricane was raging, but although I saw trees uprooted beneath me, a bit of wadding remained unmoved where I had placed it on this board," touching the one on which the instruments were arranged.

"Azackly, miss, I unnerstan'," he responded, with an air that said, "I can't quite swaller that crammer."

"But indeed, Captain Potter, I am only stating a fact. A balloon is not like a ship, you know; it offers no resistance whatever, but yields itself entirely to the current ·impelling it. Directly I cast anchor, I feel the full force of the wind."

Shaken in his opinion, but not convinced by the aëronaut's assertion, the bluff sceptic held his peace.

Not so the expectant crowd without the works, for since the balloon had raised her head to view, large numbers had been gathering to witness the ascent, and were now signifying their impatience to those within, by groaning, hooting, and shouting.

It was close upon noon when the pipe from the gasometer to the neck of the balloon was closed, and the car attached to the hoop. All being in readiness, the aëronaut and her *compagnon de voyage* took their opposite seats in the basket vehicle.

"Dear heart alive! I be all o' a quake," exclaimed Mrs. Potter, as she convulsively grasped the hand Gytha extended her over the side. "I shall scream for sure, when I see 'ee fly up."

"Then yer had better stand back and shut yer blinkers," said her husband, with blunt pleasantry. "I wuss yer a fair voyage, miss," he added, as in his turn he gripped the supple white hand. "I doesn't know as I'd mind bein' skyward-bound myself. Must be a wery queer way o' sailin', no luffin', nor tackin', nor nothing to do but just sit and be blowed along!"

Smiling at his mistaken notion of aërial navigation, Gytha laid hold of one of the ballast-bags suspended outside the car, and in her clear voice gave the signal, "Let go."

The workmen who had been holding the ropes, simultaneously yielded their grasp, the balloonist threw out a shower of sand, and it seemed to O'Rorke as though the earth was suddenly sinking, down, down, down, leaving the balloon suspended in motionless quiescence. But, lo, hundreds of hats and handkerchiefs are being frantically waved, hundreds of voices are frantically cheering, and he began to comprehend that no earthquake had happened; but that the *Serena* had fairly started.

How rapidly dwindled the round gasometer and huddled crowd! How rapidly spread the wide panorama of land and sea! Absorbed in the novelty of his situation, he silently contemplated the strange aspect in which familiar objects were now presenting themselves to his view.

Suddenly a fog obscured his vision, and he turned his baffled eyes towards his companion. A misty figure sat in her place. He glanced upwards—the balloon was invisible ! A chilly feeling of unreality fell on him—an apprehension of witches' devices, their mist-spreading, and spell-workings. He held his breath and listened. The cheering of the multitude had died away; utter silence met his straining ears.

" What a dense cloud ! I can scarcely see you."

The sound of her voice instantly restored to him a sense of actuality.

" Yes, a total eclipse of the earth," he responded, lightly.

Rays of light, now piercing the opaqueness, apprised him that they were near the confines of the cloud-layer. A burst of dazzling light, and they soared into a sunny immensity of heavenly space. Looking upward, O'Rorke saw a glorious sweeping arch of intense blue sky; looking downward, a boundless ocean of cloud billows, rolling swiftly, silently, from east to west.

As from that frail car, suspended between heaven and earth, he looked abroad on the lifeless, soundless world of air, his soul "Received a shock of awful consciousness." It was a relief to turn to his fellow-being, and in her eyes find what that empty infinitude denied him—the response of life.

" How can you ever endure such awful silence—such absolute isolation! " he exclaimed under his breath.

" You find it oppressive? " she asked, and . there was a disappointed accent in her tone.

" Not with your companionship; but were I alone, I should find it appalling," he admitted, marvelling more than ever at her strange predilection. "I wonder how high we are?"

"Four thousand three hundred and thirty-five feet," she said, consulting the barometers. "That stratus must have been nearly two thousand feet thick. But I am forgetting the guide-rope!"

Rising from her seat, she began to work the windlass.

"You must allow me to do that," he said, rising rather apprehensively to his feet, but to his comfort he felt as secure standing as sitting.

"It is five hundred feet in length, so it will take some time running out," she said, giving place to him.

"There's no lack of ascending force," he remarked, as the *Serena* continued her upward course.

"The heat of the sun assists it. You should turn to a windlass-song," she added, watching the lessening coils of rope.

"I am sorry I know none such."

"But any would answer the purpose."

Had O'Rorke been with a brother Templar, he would have at once burst into "The Rising Barrister;" but, being a proficient in adapting himself to his company, he instead, half sung, half chanted, the following fragments :—

> "Who leads us with a gentle hand
>   Thither, O thither,
> Into the Silent Land?

> "Into the Silent Land!
>   To you, ye boundless regions
> Of all perfections!   Tender morning visions
> Of beauteous souls!"

The last coil of the rope was unwound, and staying his hand, he looked at the fair pilot. She was gazing afar with wistful intentness into the "boundless regions."

The cessation of sound recalled her.

"I could wish you had another five hundred feet to unwind, if the song must conclude with the task," she said, with a smile that united the wistfulness of her past mood with the lightsomeness of her present.

" The concert-hall is of too trying dimensions," said O'Rorke, laughing, as leaning his arms on the edge of the car, he looked down on the straight, motionless guide-rope.

The *Serena* had now yielded herself to a current, that the compass indicated to be an easterly one. " We must try to find a northerly current in a little while," said Gytha, glancing at the chronometer. Fifteen minutes had elapsed since they started.

His eyes bent on the ocean of sunlit billows, that erewhile so swiftly rolling, had appeared suddenly becalmed from the moment the *Serena* changed her course. O'Rorke reflected on the strange change of circumstances that had befallen him. But a few hours before, he had been dozing in a close, little cabin; and now into what empyrean magnificence was he exalted !

" What an atom one feels," thought he, "in such boundless immensity. It is like contemplating Eternity—staggering, overwhelming ! " Then, looking down on his fair companion, he said, " How motionless the clouds appear; now there's no visible sign of the wind, it is almost impossible to believe that there is any. The *Serena* seems sailing as miraculously as the ship in Coleridge's legend. Fancy an aërial Ancient Mariner; one doomed to drift on, and on, over this boundless ocean, from the east to the west, from the north to the south ; ever listening to never-broken silence; ever watching for, but never sighting any shape or sign of life.

> ' Alone, alone, all, all, alone,
> Alone on a wide, wide sea.' "

" No, I won't try to fancy anything so morbid ! " said Miss Keppel, smiling, and looking up at the speaker with eyes no longer shadowed with serious thought, but brilliant with exuberant vitality. "Doubtless, they so shone," thought O'Rorke, "when last night she

> 'Could not chain
> Her spirit; but sailed forth under the light
> Of shooting stars.'"

"I shall be afraid to mount higher," she went on, "since you are so morbidly inclined at this altitude. I shall rather be trying for a favourable current below."

"That my dense mind may find its equilibrium," he rejoined; "but, seriously, I hope you won't think of descending; my whole being is rejoicing in the white splendour beneath—the blue sublimity above us. How I should like to behold this celestial world in all its different aspects—when sunset and sunrise are transfiguring 'these air-born shapes.' When the moon is on high, flooding all space with her divine radiance; or when the stars are shining and the red meteors shooting—which you probably beheld last night."

" Not until the *Serena* carried me above the cloud-layer, when I was struck by the great number and intense brilliancy of the stars, and while I was watching, two meteors fell simultaneously in parallel courses."

" You should have availed yourself of the opportunity to descend 'In a star-parachute,' as Blanchard wished he could."

" Did he ever express such a fanciful wish as that ? " she asked.

" I am speaking of Blanchard the poet, not Blanchard the aëronaut," he explained,

" I cannot say I am as well acquainted with the poetry of the one as I am with the exploits of the other," she said. " It is very seldom poets make ballooning their theme. I must get his works. In which poem does that scientific conceit occur ? "

" A fancy piece, 'Leisure and Love.' But you must not expect him to treat of aërostation. Still I think you would admire some of his delicate rhapsodies on clouds. He was a Yarmouth man, you know ; and a friend of mine told me he— Land Ho ! " he broke off.

Springing to her feet, she looked eagerly with him overboard, and through a tunnel-like opening in the cloud, caught a glimpse of green fields. The next moment the clouds commingling, destroyed the fairy vista.

" I shall be on the alert for that cloud to wink again.   Ah ! your posy ! " he exclaimed.

In leaning over the side of the car, her knot of chrysanthemums had become loosened and had fallen overboard.

" They are all eagerness to return to their mother-earth," observed O'Rorke, watching the scattered and falling flowers ; " but no—they hang back, they parley together.   ' Let us tarry here ! ' say they, ' earth hath not sunshine so bright, or dew so sweet ! ' "

" Indeed, they are not hanging back ! " said Gytha, smiling, " It is an optical illusion on your part."

" Ah, they have vanished ! " exclaimed O'Rorke, as the flowers drowned themselves in the cloud.

" And we have risen thirty-five feet, in consequence of their desertion," she announced, comparing the barometers.

" Never ! " he exclaimed, incredulously, " I had no idea we were so delicately counterpoised ! You should carry dewy flowers for ballast, instead of arid sand."

" I think it is time to discharge some of the 'arid sand,' and mount in search of Boreas," she said, with a light smile, thrusting her hand into a ballast-bag. On her discharging the handful of sand the balloon reassumed a vertical course.

Alternately consulting the compass and barometer, she continued to throw out ballast, until the former indicated that the

Serena had penetrated into a north-east current, and the latter, that she had reached an altitude of eight thousand four hundred feet.

The clouds could now be seen moving far below in a transverse direction— moving in refulgent beauty and dreamy silence.

" Certainly, aërial travelling is supremely charming ! " O'Rorke observed.

" Yes ; and it is a pity such a prejudice exists against it.   It cannot be so perilous as is generally supposed, for it is computed that out of ten thousand ascents, only fifteen lives have been lost."

" At that rate, it cannot be so hazardous as some other modes of locomotion. I presume your adventures have been, on the whole, fairly free from danger."

" The greatest danger that ever threatened me was when I was with my father, nearly eight years since. I remember it was on my fourteenth birthday.

During the ascent, we met with a slight fall of snow : later on, the rarefaction of the air caused a dilation, and when my father attempted to open the valve, he found it would not act. It was ice-sealed. We had no sooner made the discovery, than we heard reports like the discharge of a pistol. I saw in a moment by my father's face that something was going wrong. On my asking him what caused the sounds, he told me he feared the netting was giving way. He had scarcely spoken when there was quite a volley of reports. On looking up into the envelope we saw what had happened. The network had broken at the top, and the balloon was pushing its way up through the widening rent. It was evident it would soon escape altogether, leaving us to be dashed to the earth, five thousand feet below."

"What a desperate situation ! But I interrupt."

"It *was* desperate ! Death seemed

inevitable. My dear father made a last effort to open the valve. But it remained immovable; so, giving up the attempt, he said there was one chance of escape for me. He would secure me to the valve-rope, so that when the envelope freed itself, it would bear me with it; and raising me to his shoulder, he tied the rope—which was fortunately a long one—around me.

"I shall never forget the agony of hanging there, listening to those ominous reports—watching the distance slowly increase between my father and myself—waiting for that terrible parting! I was turning giddy with the thought of seeing him precipitated into space, when I was violently jerked. I thought the awful moment had come. But he cried out, 'The ice has broken! The valve is open!' Instantly we began to descend. Springing up into the hoop, my father released me, and let the valve close, as we were descending with too great rapidity. The danger of the balloon escaping was now greater than ever; but in two minutes we were safe on a grassy hill-slope."

"That was a narrow escape! You must have found it difficult to realize your safety!" said O'Rorke, who had been listening to her with the greatest interest. Then looking up at the shapely sphere, he asked, "Is this the balloon that caused you such an agony of fear?"

"Oh, no; the *Serena* is only four years old. That was the *Lilian*, she was destroyed by fire three years after. The barn in which she was kept was found one morning burnt to the ground. Our regret over the *Lilian* was, however, quickly followed by horror at the discovery that Thrupp was buried under the ruins. He lived in a cottage near, and seeing the fire had made an attempt to rescue the balloon. He was still living, but fearfully burnt.

The doctors gave no hope of saving his life, for the top of his head was completely charred. But one of them, knowing there was a French surgeon then in London who had made himself famous by his successful cranial operations, invited him to a consultation. He came, expressed his belief that recovery was possible, and performed an operation that was considered a miracle of surgical skill. He removed the entire cranium, and then protected the brain with an artificial covering, until a membrane formed over it."

"But surely the man's reason was not preserved?"

"Yes, I am thankful to say he lost none of his faculties. Poor Thrupp! It was a shock to him at first to know that he had lost his skull; but he soon became rather proud, than otherwise, of the fact. And certainly M. d'Arminges was proud of the cure. He said—"

"D'Arminges? Why, he is my brother-in-law! And I have been thinking how much he would have liked to have the case come under his eye and hand!"

"Your brother-in-law! Oh, I am pleased! My father and he used to correspond, and since then I have often wished I could hear of him, especially since Paris has been besieged. Is he still there?"

"Yes, my sister tried hard to prevail on him to leave it. But he would not hear of that when it was probable he would be so much needed there. Then, of course, she wished to remain with him, and it was only out of consideration for their little boy's safety that she was at length induced to go to Mrs. Cumberland, a cousin of ours, in London. In a letter Fanny, my sister, received from him a few days before I left, he said the number of wounded was terribly on the increase. I fear, though, it will be long before she hears from him again, unless he avail himself of the aërial posts. That was a bold venture of Duruof's. How enraged the Prussians must have been when he soared over their heads, and sent down his *cartes de visite.*"

"They must indeed. I was so amused when I read the account," she said, her sparkling eyes showing her sympathy with the venturesome Frenchman. "Doubtless M. d'Arminges will take advantage of that resource. Your sister must be very anxious."

"Extremely. I saw in yesterday's paper the investment was completed, and who knows when that 'iron girdle' will be broken? There is no saying to what extremity the siege may be pushed. It was most unfortunate that Jules Favre's interview with Bismarck ended so unsatisfactorily."

"I must open the valve for a moment," she said, rising. "The gas is dilating.

And besides, I think it is time we descended below the clouds, so that we may find out our whereabouts. Jumping up, O'Rorke offered to pull the rope for her. Declining his offer, she told him to look up into the envelope, and he would see two crescents of light appear. So peering up into the silken, semi-dark dome, he waited for the valve-lids to open.

Half a minute passed, and yet no light gleamed.

"*It will not act!*"

The alarming exclamation had scarcely left her lips, when O'Rorke's hands grasped the rope, just above hers, on which the blue veins were vividly defined, by reason of her tight grip.

"May I try?" he asked, looking anxiously at her blanched, upturned face.

"Oh, yes!" she eagerly replied, and waited in watchful suspense while he applied his strength cautiously.

But no yielding of the rope, no glimmering of light marked his efforts. In a few moments impatience replaced caution, and he exerted his whole strength on the stubborn rope. Suddenly he found himself on his knees. The rope had broken midway! Half was jerked down into the car, the other half swung to and fro, far up in the globe.

Speechless with consternation, he looked up into her face. But she did not meet his look, her dismayed eyes were intent on the hanging rope.

" Good Heavens ! what have I done ? "

" Do not blame yourself," said Gytha, " the rope was of no use since it would not make the valve act. What *can* be amiss with it ? " she added, looking up at the dark metallic circle. " I wish we had discovered it was unmanageable before we mounted above the clouds. There are none here to cause a condensation." She looked up apprehensively at the balloon. It was dilating into a shape that warned her how great was their peril.

"Is there *nothing* I can do ? Are there no means by which we could sink into the clouds ?" he said, looking down on the cloudy haven where they would be.

"The only thing is to make incisions. It is a dangerous expedient; but unless the gas finds some vent it will burst the balloon," she said, with alarm in her rapid tone and quick gesture, as she took up a knife and thrust it into her companion's hand.

Swinging himself up into the hoop, O'Rorke raised his outstretched arm to make an incision ; but a loud hissing noise stayed his hand.

The gas had made a vent for itself, in the upper portion of the balloon, which at once began to collapse, and consequently to descend, with a rapidity that told them how great was the outrush of gas.

Springing down from the hoop, O'Rorke

joined in Gytha's desperate efforts to lighten the car with all possible dispatch.

"Cut the grapnel-rope!" she directed, as she hastily unhung the ballast-bags.

Still the velocity of their downfall seemed in nowise moderated.

Glancing at the barometer, Gytha saw they were now four thousand seven hundred feet distant from the earth. At the same moment the *Serena* plunged into the clouds, and, owing to their condensing influence, her precipitant descent was sensibly augmented.

"Throw out anything—everything!" she said, suiting her action to her order.

Down, down whirled the balloon through the gloomy region of cloud—a very Valley of the Shadow of Death. And now a blurred mass of green seemed to be rushing up to meet the travellers, and hasten the inevitable collision.

Having thrown out every movable

article of weight, Gytha and O'Rorke
stood mute and motionless, their eyes
tensely fixed on verdant gardens, about
which people were wildly rushing.
Suddenly Gytha's white lips parted to
give vent to a sharp cry, as a dark leaping
form crossed her vision, and with a light-
ning flash of comprehension she knew that,
to diminish her danger, her companion
had resigned his chance of escape.

CHAPTER V.

" Death rides on every passing breeze,
He lurks in every flower ;
Each season has its own disease,
Its peril every hour ! "

Heber.

THE mental shock was almost immediately followed by a bodily one ; the car striking the ground with great force threw Gytha headlong out, close by a pile of stripped hop-poles. For half a minute she lay prone; men, women, and children crowding round her, agape with awe. Before any one of them had summoned up courage to do aught but gape, Gytha had staggered to her feet. With dazed eyes she looked around at the strange faces of the surrounding crowd, that was rapidly increasing, to the diminution of a ring of people a few rods off.

"A good job she ain't killed too!" said one of these fresh arrivals, a brawny man, with a bill-hook in his hand. As the words fell on Gytha's ear, her eyes, quickening into alarmed comprehension, went straight to the distant ring, and she started forward; the crowd making way for her with one accord. Followed by a large number, she hastened with stumbling precipitancy towards the distant knot of spectators—spectators of what?

The next minute, breathless and panting, she had forced her way through the ring of spectators, and, as her straining eyes fell on a bloodstained, upturned face, a long and bitter wail broke from her lips.

"Is he killed?" she gasped, throwing herself on her knees beside the prostrate figure, opposite a gentleman, or rather yeoman, who was doing his best to ascertain if any of O'Rorke's bones were broken.

" No, no ! Don't you hear him breathing ? " he said, in a subdued voice.

Yes, in truth, she could hear him now—breathing so heavily that her fears told her he was dying.

" Let me," she said hastily, as the yeoman attempted with his huge fingers to unfasten the dainty necktie. While her trembling hands sought to accomplish the task, the yeoman raised the closed eyelids of the injured man, and critically watched the fixed pupils of the eyes that seemed to her already glazing in death.

" All the symptoms of compression," muttered the yeoman, as he closed the rigid eyes.

" Can you do nothing for him—are you a doctor ? " she asked, in a tone of sharp urgency.

" No; though I have some knowledge of surgery. But I have sent for one. As far as I can ascertain there are no broken bones, so we will not delay his removal to the house."

And he gave sundry directions to certain of the men standing by. While Gytha looked down on the set face, her eyes reflected a fearful doubt as to whether vital expression had not vanished for ever.

The next minute there was a slight commotion among the bystanders, occasioned by the arrival of a hop-bin, that had undergone a hasty adaptation to serve as a stretcher.

Rising to her feet, Gytha anxiously watched the removal of the death-like figure.

Four stout labourers moved forward with their burden, whilst their master turned to Gytha and offered his arm, saying, " The house is some distance off; I hope you feel equal to walking it."

" Thank you, yes; I do not need assistance," she said, and her words were confirmed by her steady gait, as they followed the tramping bin-bearers.

On the way they passed the crowd pressing round the heap of silk and net-work. Eyeing, fingering, smelling—never was object of wonder more curiously investigated.

"Here, you idlers! Your fingers would be better employed picking the bines, than that stuff! Back to the bins with you, one and all," shouted the yeoman. And there was an immediate, albeit reluctant, movement to obey his orders.

Modifying his stentorian voice, he turned and questioned the balloon-wrecked stranger at his side, as to the cause of the accident.

"I must have a look at that piece of machinery," he said, on hearing it was owing to the valve's refractoriness. "I wonder your companion did not make sure that his balloon's apparatus was in perfect working order, before he ventured to take you with him. Having endangered your life, he could not do less than take the leap, ugly as it was ! ”

“ But Mr. O’Rorke was not responsible. It is my balloon ; and I have never before known the valve to be out of order,” she answered.

“ *Your* balloon ! ” he exclaimed, astonishment augmenting his habitual force of tone, “ and under your sole management ? ” he questioned, with a knitting of his brows that said as plainly as words, “ Then no wonder things went wrong.”

“ I am thoroughly experienced in aëronautics,” she replied, somewhat shortly ; “ but when I ascended last night, it was only with—”

“ What, have you been up since last night ? ” he interrupted, startled out of all ceremony.

She flushed deeply at his abrupt question, and hastened to speak of the accident of the previous night, her enforced descent

into the North Sea, and timely rescue by
Mr. O'Rorke.

"So he was unknown to you twelve
hours ago," he commented. "Do you
know his address—in case we should have
to telegraph to his people? He is not
married, I suppose, or he would have set
more value on his life!"

"Oh, no!—at least, I think not. He has
a sister, but I do not know her address.
And he mentioned an uncle, but all I know
of him is that he bears the same name, and
lives in Dublin."

"That's not very definite. Did he
happen to mention his business or pro-
fession?"

"Yes, he told me he was a law student
of the Inner Temple."

"Then we can apply there for his
uncle's address, in case of emergency."

Returning to the point at which he had
interrupted her, she told him how, on
reaching Yarmouth, O'Rorke had under-

taken the removal of the *Serena* to the gas-works; thus it was that she had omitted to examine the valve.

"I shall never forgive myself the neglect," she concluded, her eyes intent on the extemporized stretcher.

Through sylvan alleys of bine-entwined poles, bending beneath the weight of thick golden clusters, they followed the four steadily-plodding labourers. Once their master bade them halt; but neither he nor Gytha could see any change in the aspect of the pallid face.

At last they emerged from the pleasant, mellow hop-gardens into sloping meadow-land, on which the September sunshine lay broad and fair. Down in the vale below, on their left, there flowed in quiet beauty a glancing rivulet; while high on their right, an extensive *hanger* displayed its luxuriant autumn-tinted leafage. Beneath the shadow of its wing there nestled a house of cottage-like picturesqueness.

The only approach to it from below was a bridle-way ; and up this the men slowly bore their burden. The yeoman now started on in advance of them, in order to open a gate that gave admittance to the hedge-enclosed garden. A gravel path wound from thence to the whitened threshold, on which was standing a tall, upright old lady, evidently on the alert for their arrival.

Her vigilant eyes betokening the keenest alarm, she hastened down the path.

" Is it all ready, mother ? " asked the yeoman.

" Yea, Mark, the corner bedroom," she answered, in a voice that, though mellowed with age, was as decisive as his own. " Hath he recovered consciousness ? "

Answering her in the negative, he motioned her towards Gytha, and preceded the men into the house.

" This is a lamentable ending to thy

pleasuring, madam," she said, with a somewhat distant air.

"It is terrible—torturing!" Gytha answered excitedly.

"Nay, madam; be comforted. Possibly he is but stunned. Doctor Cobbold will, I hope, be here before long." And thus speaking she conducted her into the main passage, from which there branched several others. Down one of these the men were moving with due wariness, there being but bare passing-room for the bin.

"Mother, we shall want you here!" called Mark, who was lending a guiding hand.

"Pray, enter and rest thyself, madam; I will return immediately," said the old lady, whose dress, as well as speech, denoted her to be a Quakeress. Leaving the door ajar, she hastened to render assistance to the injured man.

In a few minutes a short, thick-set gentleman, somewhat advanced in years, arrived at the house, and was immediately conducted by a neat maid-servant down the narrow passage, and up the three steps that led to the corner bedroom.

After a long interval, he reappeared, accompanied by the mistress of the household.

"And now, friend Cobbold, wilt thou step in and speak to this venturesome girl?" she said, leading the way to the door she had left ajar.

Before he could make reply, there was a hasty movement in the room; the door was quickly opened, and there stood, not the modified tight-rope dancer of the doctor's imagination, but a pale, anxious-looking young gentlewoman, as sober in her attire as her Quakeress hostess.

"What a splendid skeleton she would make! She is symmetry itself!" he thought.

> "A bow of sleek devotion
> Engendering in his back."

A bow that was, however, startled out of a graceful consummation by the impetuous outburst of Gytha,—

" Will he live ?   *Does* he live ? "

" He *does* live.   But as yet, madam, I cannot assert—he *will* live," he answered sententiously.

" Is he conscious ? "

" Conscious, no !   We must not expect consciousness to return so quickly after so violent a concussion."

" Tell me, what is it—his head ? " she asked.

" Yes, my dear madam, I grieve to say my examination leads me to conclude he has sustained fracture of the skull.   I have telegraphed to Sir Vincent Hunt, requesting his attendance."

Her face blanched.

" Will he die ? " was the question that came faltering from her parched, white lips.

" No, no !   Brain fever is the worst we need fear.   Pray sit down and try to be calm, madam. We must be glad his case admits of hope. Eh, Mrs. Orde?" he added, turning to the old lady, who was busy at a table on which untouched refreshments were spread.

"Truly, friend Cobbold, glad and thankful I am," she said, returning with a cup of tea, which she placed on a small table at Gytha's side. "Do drink this, madam, it will steady the nerves."

"Quite right, Mrs. Orde. And then a spell of sleep is what she needs."

"Exactly, doctor." Then turning her steady eyes on her guest, she said, "I have had a bedroom prepared for thee, for I have heard from my son, thou hast been turning night into day."

"You are very good, Mrs. Orde, to be so considerate; but I could not rest until I have heard the result of the consultation. How soon can Sir Vincent arrive?" she asked, turning to Dr. Cobbold.

"Here is your answer, if I mistake not,"

he said, as, throwing open the window, he beckoned to a telegraph-boy, who was making his way to the front door.

"'Send conveyance to meet the four-fifty train,'" read the doctor aloud. "And now," glancing at his watch, "it is close upon three."

Gytha started from her seat, and began pacing the room.

"Now, my dear madam, you must not excite yourself. Let me prevail on you to control your impatience, and try to get a little rest on that sofa. I must return to my patient now."

"Thou must be much shaken, madam. It would be well to rest thy body, if thou canst not thy mind," said Mrs. Orde, when the doctor had left the room, and Gytha, heedless of his injunction, continued her restless pacing, her troubled eyes gazing straight before her.

"Ask me to do anything but rest. That is impossible!" The pained accent

of her voice caused the good Quakeress
to say to herself, " Verily the girl's conscience sorely reproves her ; " and as she
watched her agitated guest, her hard face
took a kindlier, or rather, a less censorious
expression than it had borne hitherto.

" I am going into the village to seek
the service of a worthy woman, who is
experienced in tending the sick. Wilt
thou come with me ? " she asked.

Gytha eagerly accepted her proposal.
And in a few minutes they started on the
errand.

CHAPTER VI.

" Shadows are trailing,
My heart is bewailing
And tolling within
Like a funeral bell."

Longfellow.

"A very bad case of compression of the brain—from bone. The cerebral injury is serious, most serious. In fact, there is danger of its fatally affecting his reason."

As Sir Vincent Hunt phlegmatically pronounced his verdict, he saw the expectant look in Gytha's dark eyes change to one of horrified fixity.

"His reason!" she exclaimed distractedly.

. The cry of distress roused the commisseration of the two doctors. Doctor Cobbold, who appeared to be endowed with more sympathy than Sir Vincent, hastened to reassure her.

"But, my dear young lady, we are not going to let that danger frighten us. No, no; we are going to see what an operation will effect. And for my part, I am sanguine respecting its result."

In a moment, to his satisfaction, Gytha's eyes were turned eagerly on him. The next moment, to his chagrin, they reverted to the clean-shaven face of his famous colleague.

"An operation—you think an operation will save his reason?"

"I hope it may be successful; but I cannot say I anticipate further than the preservation of life."

Discouraging as was his answer, the hopeful eagerness did not disappear from his listener's face; but rather increased, as she said hurriedly,—

" Then M. d'Arminges—he must see him ! He will save his reason ! "

" M. d'Arminges, humph, the French specialist," said the English one, thoughtfully.

" And Mr. O'Rorke's brother-in-law," quickly added Gytha.

" Then we must consult him by all means. There is no immediate necessity for the operation, but consciousness will remain suspended until it does take place. I will communicate with him at once ; but stay—is not M. d'Arminges attached to the Salpêtrière ? "

" He is," she answered promptly.

" And the Salpêtrière is in Paris," he said, with laconic significance.

" *Paris !* Wheugh, then M. d'Arminges is about as accessible as the man in the moon," lamented Dr. Cobbold, with genuine regret. The prospect of being one in a consultation that included the famous French surgeon had been highly attractive to the ambitious little man.

"But he is accessible!" she said, with animated decision. "I can fetch him in my balloon. I must telegraph to Thrupp to come down at once. He will be able to repair the valve. In the meantime I must get the envelope mended."

Three pairs of eyes focussed themselves on her flushed, earnest face.

Sir Vincent was the first to speak.

"My dear girl! you cannot consider— you forget the Prussian bullets. A pretty target your balloon would make."

"I shall provide myself with plenty of ballast, so as to be able to surmount that danger."

"And what if you find yourself blown out to sea, or into the enemy's country?" pursued the surgeon.

"I cannot let such bare contingencies as those deter me," she said decisively.

"Foolish, infatuated girl! Thou wouldst not surely again endanger the life so mercifully spared to thee?" sternly questioned the old Friend, from where she stood by the open cupboard, in which she had been delving with hospitable intent, when Gytha's proposal had arrested her attention.

"Yes, preserved to me, through his sacrifice. I owe my life to him," was the low-toned reply.

"A debt you may pay, and he be none the better off," said Sir Vincent. "You had better remain here, safe on earth, and let me do my best for him. Or if you would like further advice—"

"No, no," she interrupted, "I must fetch M. d'Arminges. I feel confident that he can save him. He has saved life and reason, when both were despaired of." And she briefly related Thrupp's case to him.

"I heard something of that case at the time," he commented. "The medical papers were full of it. He is, without doubt, a peerless operator, and it is strangely unfortunate his skill cannot benefit his own relative."

"But it shall! I must and will make the attempt. If I fail, if you do not soon hear from me—then perform the operation. And heaven guide your hand!"

The silence that followed her fervent ejaculations was broken by the clink of glass from the cupboard, that was again engulphing the Quakeress's snowy cap— a clink that sounded most suggestive and pleasant in Doctor Cobbold's puffy little ears. Then, thinking it high time he vocalized his presence, he turned and addressed Gytha,—

"But, my dear young lady, I understood your aërostat was blown to tatters."

"Oh, no ; it was only a rent, a tailor can quickly mend it. Perhaps you can recommend me one ?"

"Why, it so happens that I have a

journeyman tailor on my premises—" he paused suddenly, bit his lip, and cast an involuntary glance at Sir Vincent's perfectly-fashioned habiliments. " I employed him out of charity, the fellow came harassing me for a job, so I asked my housekeeper to give him some odds and ends of household mending. His handiwork suffices well enough for that, and would, I have no doubt, answer your requirements."

"Thank you. A few yards of firm stitching is all I require."

" Then I will send round for him; my house is close by. Doubtless Mrs. Orde will lend me her good Jonah's legs for the purpose."

" Certainly, friend Cobbold," said the Quakeress ; and, moving to a panel in the wall, she raised it, disclosing a glimpse of a kitchen, and directed a domestic to send in Jonah.

In a minute a puny boy, neatly clad

in grey homespun, appeared before the assembly.

"Jonah, look attentively at this gentle-man, and attend to the directions he will give thee."

Thus exhorted by his mistress, the lad fixed his wandering gaze on the doctor's full-blown physiognomy.

"Now, Jonah, my boy, where do I live?"

"Nigh by Murray's mills, sir, in the house with the goggles."

"Goggles!" repeated the doctor, sur-prised in his turn.

"Yea, sir, the goggles, with water running from them."

"Gargoyles, Jonah, gargoyles," said his mistress, correcting him

"Bless me! I've been told my house possesses a commanding view; but this is the first time I've been told it possesses an afflicted vision," and the little doctor laughed until he was fain to wipe his own watering orbs.

"Well, my man, run as fast as you can to the house with the 'goggles,' and say the doctor requires Long John immediately at—shall I say here, madam, or the hop-grounds?"

"The hop-grounds. The tissue can better be mended where it lies, and it will save time for him to go there at once."

Gytha's quick tone caused a suspicion to break on him, that she had been more irritated than entertained. And turning to Jonah, he hastily despatched him.

"And this Thrupp, Miss Kepple," began the surgeon, putting in his pocket the note-book in which he had been making jottings, "he will, of course, accompany you?"

"Yes, as far as Rouen. An old friend of my father, himself an aëronaut, lives there, and will, I am sure, facilitate my ascent."

"In that case, Rouen is an advantageous starting-station, else I should have advised your choosing one nearer Paris.   But why make the ascent alone?   Do you think the man will hold back?"

"No, Sir Vincent, quite the reverse; but there is no necessity whatever for the risk being doubled.   I am used to manage alone."

"But you would probably find him of great service when you get there."

"Paris is not a strange city to me; I have often been there with my father. And descend where I will, I have never yet missed respect. The comfort of Thrupp's services would not compensate the discomfort of knowing at what risk he rendered them, for if he went with me he would be obliged to remain in Paris until the siege is over, as the *Serena* cannot carry more than two."

"Well, well, I suppose you know best," he said, relapsing into his neutral tone.

"But I shall need him to take charge of her as far as Rouen.   I must telegraph

to my aunt at once," she said, producing
a pocket-book and taking from thence a
telegram-form.

"May I give it in for you?" he asked.
"I am bound for the station in a few
minutes. I have some cases in town that
I must attend to, but I will run down
again early to-morrow."

Thanking him, she hastily pencilled,—

"G. Keppel,   Mrs. Colborne,
    Tenacres,   Rutland Lodge,
      Chilworth.   Chelsea.
Safe, and with friends. Met with balloon
accident. Require Thrupp and reserve
instruments immediately. Will write.
Please send my cheque-book and travel-
ling-bag."

The sinking sun was pointing a fiery
ray, as a finger in scorn, through the
screening vine-foliage, at the torn, shape-
less groveller that, when at his zenith,
he had beheld boldly invading his airy
dominions. The ray was presently inter-

cepted and dazzlingly reflected, by the gigantic brazen thimble encompassing the crown of a battered chimney-pot hat covering the head of a moody, jaundiced-looking individual, nearly buried beneath the silken tissue on which he was plying his needle.

Occasionally the fellow would lift his heavy eyes to cast a glance of sluggish interest, across the undulating expanse of material, at the earnest face of his new employer standing on the other side, intent on cutting out various sized patches of oil-skin, which she severally handed to the yeoman standing near, who forthwith applied them to the impaired silk.

After awhile, from under his red eyelids, the tailor saw the huge yeoman, together with his companion, come slowly round towards him.

"I hope the light will outlast your task, John," said a deep voice, as the herculean figure halted.

"Can't say. The stuff's tough enough, I can tell yer *that*. It's turned the points o' three dratted needles," he grumbled, never lifting his eyes.

"Yes, it must be very tiresome. It is the varnish that has so hardened the silk," said Gytha, noting with dismay the lengthy rent that the plodding needle must yet traverse. "But as I told you, you shall be well paid for your trouble," she added, desirous of inciting the dull-browed malcontent to some dexterity.

"Glad to hear it," he said stolidly. "The mean old cove I've been jobbin' for ain't too ready to fork out his tin. 'E were for dockin' me o' my drop o' beer, 'cause I cut 'is coat-tails a shavin' too short. But I soon let 'e see I weren't agoin' to stand that. Talkin' o' beer, my gullet's as parched as this 'ere stuff," he added, raising his mumbling voice, in order that his hint should be the better conveyed to the hop-grower, who was following Gytha to where she now stood bending over a small heap of recovered, but more or less injured, instruments.

"I'm going down to the village, and will send you up a tankard," said Mark, looking back over his shoulder.

"I fear they are all useless," he remarked, subduing his voice to the delicate ear he now addressed, as he looked down regretfully on the broken thermometer which Gytha held in her hand.

"Fortunately I have a reserve set at home, that I have desired Thrupp to bring with him," she said, putting down the ivory wreck, and taking up a bruised speaking-trumpet.

"That is indeed fortunate, for I doubt if any shop in Chilworth could supply you with instruments of that rare make. That reminds me—I must be off for the rope and varnish. But in the meantime you will get tired standing about."

"Then I can rest here," she said, pausing by a pile of stripped hop-poles.

Quick as thought, he spread thereon an overlooked poke.

"That was a convenient oversight," he said, looking round on her with a smile. To his wonder, she met his glance with a look of painful abstraction. She was thinking of how O'Rorke had draped the fish-crate.

The expression lingered long on her face, as she sat gazing with pondering fixity at the thimble-crowned hat in the distance.

Now and then a bird twittered close by her, or a white moth sped by on the soft evening air. Purple clouds gathered in the west, and slowly shadowed the delicate apple-green stretches of sky; and, as slowly, the light passed from field and meadow. Twilight gradually possessed the land, deepening away to the horizontal band of dark blue mistiness, where but a few moments since a belt of pines had stood blackly traced against the now vanished rose-radiance.

When Mark Orde returned, bearing in one muscular hand a jar labled Linseed Oil Varnish, and in the other a coiled pack of rope, he found Gytha standing near the balloon in earnest discussion with an undersized, odd-looking character, whom no one could look at and fail to be struck with his resemblance to an otter. Receding forehead, small bright eyes, sharp prominent nose, each feature instinct with alertness, and a slender little body, that seemed to wriggle with disputative agitation as he talked, all combined to render the resemblance striking and unique. Orde soon learned from Gytha that her eager, little interlocutor, who evidently ill-brooked his interruption, was no other than Thrupp.

"I cannot convince him of the advisability of his remaining in Rouen," she added.

"I's be suner convinced ane ee[1] is better nor twa," he asserted, in a shrill treble. " I wad rather gang to Paris wi' ye, an I hae to eat horse and donkey to my deeing day. I am a' asteer to wauff my cap to the German chaps!" And in the excitement of the anticipation, he plucked off and waved aloft his Scotch cap, leaving to view a brown silk skull-cap.

" But, Thrupp, I have been counting on you to relieve me of the *Serena* when M. d'Arminges and I come out of Paris, and if you are left behind there, I shall be obliged to trust her to strangers, and who can say how roughly she may be treated."

She did well to represent the case in this light, since he held the welfare of the *Serena* second only to her own.

" Weel, weel, I maun bide in Rouen," he

---

[1] *Scot.*, eye.

said resignedly; "but I's hae nae peace of mind 'till I set een on ye agin," he added in an undertone, as he darted off to the alamort tailor, and in less than a minute was seated in his stead, stitching away with an aptitude that showed needle and thimble were no strangers to his fingers.

Having vented some of his resentment by cuffing the pot-boy, who, forgetful of his vocation, had been hanging round the balloon, the displaced journeyman shambled up to his employer, and whined a hope that he was not "agoin' to be done out o' his due;" he had done his job all but a few stitches, when "that imp" snatched it out of his hand.

For answer Gytha handed him a half-sovereign. He eyed the coin with a decidedly brightened aspect, turned it over in his palm, spat on it, and with a mumbled "Thank'ee miss," he thrust it in his pocket and went on his way, the same as that taken by the pot-boy.

The hop-grower's face took a vexed expression as he watched the retreating figure.

"I was so glad to see Thrupp. It seemed as though that man would *never* finish his task," she said, regarding with relief the busy stitcher.

"That little fellow certainly seems worth two of him. Has he been able to enlighten you at all respecting your balloon's escape?"

"Yes, he has just been telling me that, after he went back into the house, a strong presentiment that something was going wrong with the balloon urged him to return. On his way there he was alarmed to see the *Serena's* light suddenly soar up and disappear, and running to the spot of ascent, he found Shootoo, the monkey, dancing around the machinery, brandishing a knife."

"That animal should be destroyed."

"Oh, I could not hear of that! My

father used to be so amused to watch his tricks.   I have agreed to Thrupp's request, that he may be kept under restraint."

"And a very wise request. The brute will be committing. murder next. I feel so vexed when I think how his devilry has caused all this trouble," he said, looking lugubriously away at the fading landscape.

"I am afraid Thrupp will not have light enough to see what is wrong with the valve," she said, as, presently turning her head, she saw that he had risen, and was stooping over the refractory machine.

"I gave directions before we started, that a muster of lanterns should be brought here as soon as the light failed," he said. "And here they come!" as he caught sight of moving distant lights.

When, some while later, Gytha stood near a lantern elevated on a pole, gazing dejectedly away into the far-stretching, deepening darkness, and listening to the sough of distant trees, her last night's sojourn on board the fishing-smack was again brought vividly to her mind.

Whilst she recalled the pleasant voice of her late companion, her reverie was abruptly terminated by Mark Orde saying something about returning to the house.

She was startled, and bitterly reminded that O'Rorke was not by her side, but lying helpless on the brink of insanity.

" There is no further need of you here," he went on, "and it would be well to rest all you can. It is half-past seven now, so you have two hours' respite before you."

He strove to speak cheerfully, but the pallor of her face depressed him greatly.

" Yes, I will return to the house," she said, with a weary look that prompted him to make one more attempt to induce her to give up the enterprise.

But when reaching the whitened threshold, he stood aside for her to enter, his downcast look affirmed both the failure of his attempt and the fixed character of Gytha's resolve to go forth on her venturous journey by land, sea and air, on behalf of the man who twice had risked his life to save her own.

CHAPTER VII.

"All holy angels keep me in this hour!
Spirit of her who bore me, look upon me!"
Longfellow.

THROB. Throb. Throb.

It seemed to Gytha, as she sat in the cabin of the packet, that the pulsating machine so near her must be sharing in the excitement, stirring her heart, and co-operating with her in the work she had determined to carry out.

Her giddy, overwrought brain craved for the respite of sleep. Once she closed her aching eyes, but "the balls like pulses beat," refusing to be lid-pent. Wearily they reopened and fell on the hard-featured, expressionless woman, indefatigably crocheting, sitting opposite.

Slowly but surely expanded the fantastic doily; no knot offered interruption. The ivory crotchet-needle journeyed round its circuit evenly as the hand of a clock. Gytha watched its smooth, fascinating progress, until the regular motion of the little ivory wand seemed to soothe her senses, and laid them under the charm of slumber.

"We have reached Dieppe, ma'am," were the words of the stewardess, aided by a touch on the arm, that broke the spell.

Gytha started to her feet. The indefatigable crochet-worker had disappeared, together with the pack of "poor, suffering humanity" that had been making such demands on the services of the stewardess. Thanking the woman, she hastened up the companion-stairs. Reaching the deck, she found to her vexation that the rain was falling heavily. Alas, for her ascent, should it continue!

Thrupp was standing just outside the hatchway, on the alert for her appearance.

" Has it been raining long?" she asked of him.

" The best part o' the night, miss."

" And the wind?"

" It has been sou'-west, but it's turned west noo."

She shivered as the rain beat sharply in her face.

" But we maun look sharp, miss. It is drenched ye will be an ye stan' here;" and thus saying he began to elbow his way through the jostling crowd.

After a brief period of confusion, she was once again being carried swiftly along the railway, watching the slant rain deluging the fields, meadows and orchards, that followed each other in endless succession. Suddenly a beam of sunlight cheered her despondent eyes, as they peered intently through the rain-blurred window.

She let down the sash, stretched out her hand, and to her delight found that the rain had ceased.

The pure, strong air seemed sweet with earthy incense, and Gytha inhaled it with all the gratefulness of a relieved mind and reviving spirit, until the train swept into the jaws of darkness.

When it emerged from the tunnel, no glistening leafage of orchards, but the dull walls of the station of Rouen met her eyes. And there, posted on the platform near the chief exit, stood the corpulent old friend whom she had apprised by telegram of her coming. Noting the spot where he stood, Gytha quickly alighted and made her way towards it, to find her friend still firmly planted thereon, peering around in every direction. Seeing her, his frowning perplexity changed on the instant to smiling delight, and he waddled eagerly forward to meet her.

" *Soyez le bieuvenu !* Dis is *à la bonne*

heure, ma petite," he welcomed, in a muffled voice that came slowly from the fat folds of his throat. "And *la belle Serene*, vaire is she? Ve must not let ze train bear her avay."

"Ah! Thrupp will see that does not happen," she said, a smile at his kindly anxiety playing on her lips.

"Ah! ze good Trupp—he is vid you zen. Dat is *bonne.* Come zen, *ma chère,* ze *calèche* vaits vidout."

In a few minutes she was seated in the said *calèche*, near which stood a vehicle of humble character, in readiness for the balloon and car.

After waiting until the machine was safely mounted thereon by Thrupp and the driver, M. Grandpierre shook the reins held in his chubby hands, to which gentle signal the sleek bay mare promptly responded.

Gytha would fain have been silent as she was borne swiftly through the old city, so full of memories; but the numerous questions of her old friend respecting her errand demanded a reply, so that by the time her questioner turned his good *Jeanne* into the scantily-wooded, but richly-flowered grounds encircling a pretty, slightly-built *château*, he was in full possession of all the information he desired, including an outline of Gytha's adventures since leaving Chelsea. Gytha drew a quick breath as she sighted it. How happily had she and her father sojourned within those selfsame walls!

Her heart swelled with unusual emotion, when, a few minutes later, she was embraced by Madame Grandpierre, an infirm old lady of most gentle presence.

"*Ma chère*, vat a *morceau* you do eat," said M. Grandpierre, observing Gytha's small appetite, after the trio had been seated awhile at the daintily-appointed breakfast-table. "Dis is *sottise!* Out zare, *la Serene* is of *déjeuné* partaking, that she collapse not, and in here you must of *déjeuné* partake, that you collapse not. Now eat you zese truffles."

Smiling at his protest, Gytha proceeded to obey his behest, notwithstanding that the vivid recollection of the little breakfast party of the previous morning had deprived her of all desire to partake of food. " Could it be only the previous morning that she had sat with her hero at that homely table at Yarmouth ? " she sadly wondered, as she now sat at this elegant board.

Her sombre reflections were interrupted by her host's thick voice slowly articulating,—

" *Ma fois !* Vaire I in ze place of M. d'Arminges, I vould velcome you as ze angel of mercy. *Grâce à ciel !* I am not in ze place of him, or any ozer *pauvre diable* vid ze view of zeven *jours de jeûne* in ze veek ! "

The vast capacity for food, which the old gentleman was evincing, gave due weight to his thanksgiving.

"It is terrible, my heart aches for them," said Madame Grandpierre in her sweet, low voice.

"Could I not take some sacks of flour with me? Would it be possible for me to procure some without causing a delay?" and Gytha looked eagerly from one to the other.

"*Certainement, ma petite, une bonne idée!*" said M. Grandpierre approvingly. "You vould take zem in place of ze *sacs de sable?*"

"I could take a few sacks of sand. The flour would serve as reserve ballast. I do hope I shall not need to waste it."

"*Allons!* Dat vould not be a great mattoire, be-yond flouring *peut-étre*, ze outzide of a German, *au lieu* of ze inzide of a Frenchman. And zince eet is for *mes compatriotes*, you must let me eet *pourvoir.*

I vill give ze order dis ve-ree mineet," and M. Grandpierre brought his fat fore-finger emphatically down on the ivory knob of the hand-bell on the table.

" And Gytha, darling," plaintively appealed madame, who had been listening with marked attention, " would it be troubling you too much to convey a few delicacies to my friend, Madame de Segur? She is an invalid like myself."

" Certainly I will, dear madame, if you will give me her address," she readily assented, although fearing the commission would involve more or less delay.

" Many, many thanks to you, dear. I have so wished I could send her a few things, which I fear she cannot now procure. She lives in the Rue de Bac, but I will have her address attached to the articles, and then they will be quite ready for you to give to a messenger."

Monsieur, who had been giving his orders respecting the sacks of flour, turned his attention in time to hear his wife's last remark, and shrugged his portly shoulders, as he helped himself to some devilled chicken, at her implicit faith in a hungry *garçon.*

"And, my dear," she went on, her cheek slightly flushing with the excitement of the moment, "may I add a few bottles of Ratifia? It is a cordial she greatly fancies."

"But, madame, it would never exist bottled in the rarefied atmosphere; it would be pop, and vanish in a trice."

"*Comme de raison!*" impatiently re-joined M. Grandpierre. "Have I not you inform-ed, *ma chére* Lucie, ze dat zevataire zim-pel vataire, do be-come as effervescent as ze champagne."

"Ah, yes, I remember now," replied his wife. "Then I must give up that idea."

Breakfast being now concluded, she asked Gytha if she felt disposed to visit the conservatories; and on being answered in the affirmative, she summoned her *bonne*, a sturdy, elderly Breton, who noiselessly wheeled an invalid-chair into the room. Having lifted her mistress into it, the servant, according to directions, propelled it through an arched doorway into a crystal fairyland, brilliant with blooms and delicious with perfumes.

Keeping pace with her hostess's chair as it slowly moved through the bowery arcades, Gytha passed admiring comments on now this, and now that, special " *mignonne* " of her host, who, however, complained that she was *distrait*. But the complaint was quickly followed by the sympathetic excuse of the aëronaut, that *a belle Serené* was *la personne qui distrait*. And her host was right; for the apprehension of anything going amiss with the balloon, during the critical process of inflation, was never absent from her mind. She was glad when, on reaching the extent of the far-stretching conservatories, M. Grandpierre proposed that, instead of returning through them, they should straightway proceed to the scene of inflation.

The *bonne* having lightly folded a wrap around her mistress, who prevailed on Gytha to make use of a spare one, they passed out of the richly perfumed atmosphere into the *jardin de plaisance*, where the north wind was blowing freshly. The *Serena* could now be seen gracefully deporting herself in the centre of an extensive lawn, which, to qualify for the purpose of ascents, M. Grandpierre had underlaid with a huge gas-pipe, the mouth of which was now inserted in the neck of the balloon.

Leaving his guest to a *tête-à-tête* with his wife, M. Grandpierre moved away to where Thrupp was busy preparing the car.

"Aye, she is soncy enough," proudly admitted that individual, in response to the admiration excited in M. Grandpierre's mind and expressed in enthusiastic, though mixed, language.

"She is *charmant! Hélas, ma pauvre Réné!* Vid vat *élégance* she did al-zo dees-play." His thick voice became tremulous with emotion, as he descanted on his loved and lost. " *Tonnerre!* Ven on my back I did lie, and did my eyes lift, *voila!* zaire was *la perfidie* zoaring avay and avay ! "

" Whaur was it she gae ye the slip, sir ? " inquired Thrupp, who had, however, heard the story before.

"In Limoges, *mon ami,* in Limoges. Ah, *la mignonne,* she did break ze heart, ze ve-ree heart of me." And his eyes blinked with tears as they gazed at the crimson and white striped sphere gracing his lawn.

" Atweel, sir, I wadna greet ower the fause loon. It was chancy (lucky) she broke the heart, an' na' the back o' ye," drily responded Thrupp, as he swung himself out of the car. " I maun gae an' close the pipe off-hand. She is fu' enough noo," and he hastened away towards the sprightly aërostat.

Looking towards the spot where he had left his wife and guest, he perceived that the latter had disappeared, and at once hurried forward to learn the reason. Before, however, he had gained madame's side, Gytha reappeared, equipped in her hood and jacket. She looked as composed as though she only purposed taking a walk or drive ; but when, a few minutes later, on Thrupp apprising her that he had completed the *Serena's* " outreik," she turned and took her farewell of Madame Grandpierre, the icy touch of her lips betokened extreme though repressed excitement.

Bidding her maid wheel her chair nearer the balloon, madame looked wistfully on, while Gytha entered the car, outside which were rigged four sacks of sand and twelve of flour, while over the hoop were slung a brace of pheasants, destined for Madame de Segur.

"The sky is somedele lowering, I doubt we will sune lose sight o' ye miss," observed Thrupp, as he shut up the car-steps. "Belike ye will find it mair cheerfu' on tither side the clouds. Hech, the spunkie is eager enough to be awa'," he added, as the *Serena* strained at her ropes, held in the strong grasp of a quartette of gardeners.

"Yes, I must away! Good-bye, dear friends," she said, looking around on them with shining eyes.

"Good-bye, dear child, good-bye. The blessed Virgin watch over you," tearfully exclaimed madame, fluttering her hand-kerchief.

"*Bon voyage, ma petite! Les saints* escort you!" ejaculated monsieur, bowing low his uncovered head.

"Gude-speed and luck gae wi' ye, miss," said Thrupp, touching his cap.

Gytha's pale, compressed lips parted in a tremulous smile of acknowledgment; for a moment they were again tightly pressed, and then the critical command was given, "Let go!"

In an instant she was snatched up from the midst of her well-wishers. In two minutes, at a height of one thousand six hundred feet, the *Serena* paused suddenly, descended a hundred feet, and then the *château* and the watchers on the lawn appeared to glide swiftly away from beneath the aëronaut, who knew the balloon had now yielded herself to a southerly current.

Soon the *château* was a white spot in the green distance, and the City of Churches lay beneath her; swiftly the view gave place to a monotony of fields, streaked with hedge-rows, and sparsely dotted with trees.

Applying herself to work the windlass, Gytha remembered how O'Rorke had

turned it to the " Song of the Silent Land."
And as she turned the wheel a forlorn
and gloomy look deepened in her eyes.

The rope, running out to its limit, broke
the sad train of thought; and, turning
from the windlass with a deep-drawn
breath, she bent over the instrument-
board and noted the indication of needle
and column. Both were satisfactory.
Raising her stooping figure to its full
height, Gytha stood for a moment in a
motionless attitude, looking up at the
buoyant sphere. It evinced no sign either
of depression or dilation. She turned,
and, folding her arms on the edge of the
car, in one of the spaces between the
suspending ropes, she looked down on the
flying landscape. Now she was speeding
over green pasture-land, where

> " The cattle are grazing,
> Their heads never raising."

Now it was an orchard, where peasants
were busy gathering the fruit; but the

heads of the bipeds were raised, one and all, and a score of gaping eyes followed her flight. And now a village, from whence rose the ringing of a forge, the crowing of cocks, or the hum of distant traffic.

But one feature was never lost to sight—the silver-grey, smooth-flowing Seine. And while that lay beneath her eyes, she knew there was little need for looking at the compass.

For a few minutes the *Serena* pursued her course over that of a straight, dusty road, where, before a quaint little way-side inn, stood a waggon of hay, that seemed to gleam in the sunlight. The driver was in the act of quaffing the contents of a tankard, when he sighted her, and excitedly pointed her out to the inn-keeper.

Then, far in advance on the road, a well-loaded diligence could be seen pushing on its way, leaving behind it a trailing cloud of dust. In a moment the wind-borne chariot overtook the lumbering conveyance whose passengers were enthusiastically waving hats, caps, and handkerchiefs.

." *Où allez-vous, monsieur?*" shouted a masculine voice, the owner evidently labouring under the mistake that the aëronaut was of the sterner sex.

Snatching the speaking-trumpet from where it hung, she raised it to her lips and made answer,—

"*A Paris! Quelle distance y a-t-il d'ici?*" Holding her breath, she intently listened for the answer.

Faintly, but distinctly, it reached her ear.

"*Il y a cinquante milles!*"

Then, as she left the diligence behind, the driver raised a horn to his lips, and a right merry blast pierced the air, and resounded from the silken dome overhead.

Looking from the lessening cloud of dust to the chronometer, she saw that forty-five minutes had elapsed since she started, in which time, according to the information just obtained, she must have travelled thirty-six miles. If the current would but hold good, another hour would suffice to cover the remaining fifty miles.

She again looked up at the balloon. It still maintained a befitting degree of rotundity. Suddenly, the composure on the balloonist's upturned face changed to a look of alarm. Those were surely rain-drops! Yes, fast and thick they fell, crackling sharply on the surface of the silk. To prevent the balloon being drenched and weighed down with moisture, Gytha decided that she must mount above the stormy nimbus, regardless of the risk of finding an adverse current, and at once discharged the contents of a ballast-bag.

Slowly the *Serena* rose against the beating rain. The aëronaut continued to cast out pound after pound of sand, her heart misgiving her, as she remarked how slowly the quantity discharged counteracted the condensing influeuce of the seemingly limitless mass of vapour through which the balloon was ascending.

Having penetrated a thickness of 8000 feet, the balloon rose out of the fog, not, as Gytha had anticipated, into a sunny far-vaulted dome of blue sky, but into a dull, cloud-bound space, where sounded a hollow moan, that apprised her of an invisible conflict between opposed currents; but glancing at the needle, as the *Serena* resumed a horizontal course, she saw to her relief that she had not surmounted the favourable current by which she had been travelling.

The car just skimmed the ruffled surface of the cloud ocean stretching away on every side to the celestial horizon. But soon the vapoury billows gathered themselves together, and rising around the aërial craft, deeply engulfed it, obstructing the wide-spreading prospect, and producing a stifling and oppressive sensation on the voyager. Gytha tried to overcome the sensation, to reason herself into calm endurance of the murky oppression; for, unless a depression on the part of the balloon obliged her, she was unwilling to rise higher above the vapour, on account of the necessary loss of ballast, and the likelihood of encountering an adverse current, of which the moaning sound above still warned her.

Suddenly there looked down upon her, from the ominous clouds overhead, the lustreless, dull orb of day, appearing to her excited imagination as the expressionless, blood-shot eye of a lunatic. A look of horror swept over her white face, and a tremor ran through her frame. If the clouds would but again hide from her sight this awful accuser! But no; the ghastly orb continued to glare upon her, until, in a panic of nameless dread, she sank trembling and nerveless on the bench, hiding her face in her hands.

CHAPTER VIII.

"And of the Prussian missiles stood the mark ?"
Victor Hugo.

GASPING for breath, Gytha let her hands fall from her face, and straightway her panic was merged in wonder. The towering masses of vapour, dissolved into rain, fell on the right and on the left of her, forming two liquid walls, opening to the *Serena* as dry a passage as that opened to the Israelites through the Red Sea. Never before had Gytha witnessed the like, and she gazed at the strange sight with intense interest.

As she gazed, a low, rumbling sound as of distant thunder struck her ear. She listened intently; the sound continued, and seemed to rise from the clouds below.

She concluded that a thunder-storm was about to burst; but very soon her straining ears perceived that it was terrestrial, not celestial artillery.

She must be over the scene of investment!

A flush tingeing her pallid face, she glanced at the barometer, it indicated an altitude of 9800 feet. Then at the chronometer, 11·55; it wanted fifteen minutes to complete the hour that she had considered would suffice to accomplish her journey. Evidently the current had gained in velocity.

Having allowed a few minutes to elapse, that the *Serena* might get well over Paris, she opened the valve for a moment. Then, as the balloon sank into the wetting fog, Gytha leaned over the car and discharged the ballast necessary to check the acceleration of the *Serena's* downward course. To her regret, she was soon obliged to largely draw upon the sacks of flour, so marked was the condensation, so rapid the descent.

Louder and louder boomed the heavy cannonade. Keener and keener sounded the sharp discharge of musketry. Her heart leapt within her when, on breaking through the clouds, she beheld the far-extending investing lines; the grey Seine, speckled with gun-boats; the long boundary of fortifications; and beyond, a con_ fusion of domes and pinnacles, marking the city of the Seven Sieges. There lay her destination; and here, directly beneath her, the heights of St. Cloud crowned by the Prussian batteries.

She flashed a glance at the barometer, 24·7 inches, 5280 feet. As yet the *Serena* was beyond gun-shot; but, owing to the moisture through which she had passed, continued to descend rapidly, in an oblique direction, towards the river.

It was with increasing alarm that she continued to throw out pound after pound of flour; but still the balloon bent her course downward. The smoke-clouded ranks of infantry became more and more distinct. Gytha could see the soldiers pointing their rifles at the fast collapsing balloon, and could hear the bullets whizzing through the air.

With trembling hands she poured out her precious ballast. The last bag was cast away; and the *Serena* still sank, the strong current inclining her nearer and nearer to the Seine. Gytha cast a longing glance at the Bois de Boulogne on the opposite side. If only the balloon could escape the balls, and cross the river to safety!

With face white as death, but eyes intensely brilliant, she severed the grapnel-rope. The *Serena* paused, and hung motionless; and as motionless stood the aëronaut, every sense on the alert for the next movement.

It was an ascensive one.

With reviving hope she looked about her for something to throw out, and so speed the ascent. She was stooping to gather up the rug, when she suddenly started upright. A vibration had apprised her of the direful fact that the balloon was struck! A loud sighing immediately ensued. The *Serena* halted and reeled, like a stunned creature; then, still quivering and sighing, sank heavily.

In desperate haste Gytha snatched up the rug and cast it out, taking as she did so a swift survey of her situation. To all appearance the balloon was bent for the river. There was just a possibility that the wind would waft her to the further bank lined with soldiers. She must prolong the descent to her utmost power.

The empty instrument-case, and the packages of isinglass, arrowroot, and such like, intended for the invalid, followed each other pell-mell into space. She was uplifting her arm to unsling the brace of pheasants when, with a cry of anguish, she let it drop heavily at her side. A bullet had struck it! Pain, like a wave of fire, overwhelmed her, and the next instant, all cold and faint at the sight of the blood staining her sleeve, she sank to the bottom of the car. Almost immediately the car struck the ground, with a shock that seemed to wrench the traveller's arm from its socket. Stifling darkness fell upon Gytha. In her agony and terror, she cried out for light, for air!

"In one moment, madame," said some one, in tolerably good English.

There was a muffled murmur of voices, a rustling stir, and then, as the collapsed envelope was dragged aside, light and a dozen excited faces burst upon her.

"*Juste Ciel!* Madame is wounded!" exclaimed the man who had spoken first, an officer, in Chasseur uniform, who vaulted lightly—despite his advanced years—into the car, and raised her from her recumbent position to a seat on the bench. Then pulling a silver flask from his pocket, he poured some cognac into the cup and held it to her white quivering lips. While his left hand was thus engaged, his right tugged unmercifully at his iron-grey *Henri Quatre* moustache. The next minute, both left and right authoritatively waved aside the crowding soldiery.

As the human palisade fell back, Gytha breathed more freely, and was inexpressibly relieved to find she had fallen amongst the French instead of the Prussians. Then the burden of her anxiety found speech.

" M. d'Arminges—I want M. d'Arminges ! "

" He shall be informed of madame's injury without delay," was her new friend's immediate rejoinder.

" Oh, it is not for that—you know then where he is ? " she questioned, with reviving animation.

"Certainly, at the Palais de l'Industrie. He is attached to the *Ambulance Internationale*. I assumed it was on account of your arm you needed him," he added, inquiringly. Then, as slitting up the blood-stained sleeve, he bared to view the white shapeliness of her arm, disfigured midway between the elbow and shoulder by a small hole, from which the blood was slowly oozing, he declared, with serious concern, "It requires surgical treatment without loss of time!"

Gytha glanced down quickly, and as quickly averted her eyes.

"Then M. d'Arminges will see to it. Is there any available conveyance here? My business with him is most pressing!" she said, looking anxiously around. Horses there were in plenty picketed about, but the only vehicles she could see were huge ambulances and provision-waggons.

"A *voiture* could be procured for madame; but, indeed, I fear the jolting would be insufferable. I will send for M. d'Arminges to come to you."

And, as he tore into strips his fine-linen handkerchief, he gave his orders to a *Garde Mobile*, who quickly made for a picketed horse, and having untethered him, mounted and rode smartly away. Gytha tightly compressed her blanched lips, as the Chasseur officer proceeded to bandage her inflamed and bleeding arm.

"Madame is as brave to endure as to venture," he observed, as he carefully continued his task. "I much lament so intrepid a venture should have so unfortunately failed. I surmise madame met with adverse currents."

"No, they have been favourable; but about an hour after I left Rouen the rain obliged me to travel above the clouds. But for that, I should have better timed my descent," she replied, dejectedly.

"Left *Rouen!* I have been under the impression you were attempting to leave

Paris ! I never dreamed it was the destination desired by madame. I rejoice you have so far succeeded in an essay that has cost you so much suffering," he concluded, looking at her skilfully-bandaged arm, with combined regret and satisfaction.

"I would not mind that, if only the balloon had escaped being struck," she said, her troubled eyes directed to the collapsed mass of silk. "I wonder to what extent she is damaged."

"I will ascertain for madame," and swinging himself out of the car, he called some of the soldiers to assist him. Having detached the envelope, he began carefully overhauling its shrinking form. It proved to be impaired only in two places, there being in the lower portion a hole, without doubt, pierced by a cannon-ball, and in the upper portion, where it must have emerged, the hole had been strained into a rent by the escaping gas.

During the investigation one of the men

pulled out to view and held aloft the pheasants, which the officer undertook to have safely delivered at the attached address.

He then requested Gytha to allow the men to bear her in the car to his tent, where she could with more safety await M. d'Arminges. In reply to which proposal she said there was no need for her to give that trouble as she could walk. Overruling her objection, he gave the word, and the basket-chariot was carefully borne over the wheel-rutted sward. How different to the velvet smoothness which she and her father had once trod; how changed was the entire scene! Then so gay and picturesque, now so devastated by the plague of war.

On her way she passed numbers of soldiers engaged in hewing down the forest-trees, and in forming barricades across the roads.

Soon the waters of a lake gleamed upon her sight, and then its whole shimmering expanse, near which extended a line of tents. Thitherward her car-bearers directed their steps, and soon halting before one, gently deposited their burden on the ground.

The officer, who had kept pace with the men, now forestalled her attempt to let down the steps, assisted her to descend and ushered her into the roomy tent. Pulling forward a camp-chair, he begged her to be seated, and then extemporized his valise into a footstool. Having prevailed upon her to take a little Maraschino, he left her with the apology that he must return to his post.

It seemed a long, weary time that she had been sitting there, with eyes closed on the light that made her brain throb feverishly, but with ears perforce open to the loud thundering of Mont Valérian, when she heard a voice announcing, "*Là—dedans, monsieur.*" And she opened her eyes just as M. d'Arminges presented himself in the opening of the tent, looking just the same as when last she saw him, both in his attire and in the aspect of his face, excepting the addition to the former of a Red Cross insignia, and to the latter of a trim "Impérial," whose glossy jettiness rendered yet more striking tho dull whiteness of his complexion. It might be said of M. d'Arminges, that he was an embodied French rendering of the English proverb that states a surgeon should possess "an eagle's eye, a lion's heart, and a lady's hand."

"I feared *la brave Anglais* could be none other than yourself, mademoiselle; the *garde* had forgotten your name by the time he reached me. But what does it all mean? I am astonished and grieved beyond words. Surely your descent in this besieged place was by accident, not design!" he said, with as perfect a pronunciation and as rapid an utterance as though he spoke his own language.

" I am here on a most painful errand, monsieur, concerning Mr. O'Rorke," she began, as she clasped his extended hand, long-fingered and slender, whose unerring dexterity had accomplished such wonders, and would, she believed, pluck her deliverer from the brink of that horrible gulf of insanity.

" Derrick—what of him ? " he asked, with an anxiety that warned her how acutely her news would affect him, and that caused her voice to falter as she proceeded to impart it.

" We—he ascended with me yesterday, an accident happened,—we were being dashed to the ground, and he leapt from the car. His head—it is injured—Sir Vincent Hunt fears his reason may be fatally affected—but oh, you will save it ! "

" Heaven grant I may ! What is the nature of the injury ? "

" Compression of the brain."

" From fracture or rupture ? "

" From bone," Sir Vincent said. " And it is to fetch you to him that I am here. But what can we do? The balloon is useless—it was struck by a cannon-ball; we shall be obliged to wait until it is mended and refilled."

The thought of the unavoidable delay flushed her pale face. " There is no other way—you cannot obtain a pass ? " she added, looking at him with an all-absorbing anxiety.

He decisively shook his head.

" Fortunately a club-balloon leaves Paris to-night, possibly I may be able to obtain a seat in her. I will ascertain as soon as I have attended to your wound."

" Go now, go at once ! Delay may lose you a seat," she urged.

The keen black eyes meeting hers took a deliberating expression.

Gytha waited impatiently for the result of his deliberation.

"I saw Captain Droue on my way here, and he told me he believed the bullet was lodged in your arm; so I have been thinking that before I see to its extraction it would be well to get you to the Hôtel Wagram. I could then leave you to the care of Madame Raboteau, a widowed lady who was very kind to my wife when we boarded there, and will I am confident do—"

"But the balloon—the seat!" she interrupted.

"I will go at once, and return in a *voiture* to convey you to the Hôtel." As he spoke he took from his surgical-case a length of broad bandage, with which he made a sling for her arm. And having done this much for the alleviation of her pain, he no longer delayed his important quest.

When he returned, Gytha's keen suspense was relieved by the welcome intelligence that he had obtained a seat.

"I *am* thankful!" she said, fervently. "I suppose you could not have secured one for me also?"

"My dear mademoiselle, a bed is what must be secured for you! I sincerely regret your having to remain in Paris; but it is inevitable. As soon as you are sufficiently restored to travel, you may be able to obtain a pass from General Trochu. I will speak about it to Doctor Daubeny, whom I shall request to attend you. But the *voiture* is awaiting you at a short distance. Do you feel equal to walking it with my assistance?"

"Certainly," she quickly replied.

Outside the tent she accepted her friend's proffered arm, and, with swimming head and uncertain steps, gave herself up to his guidance.

In a few minutes he lifted her into the open *voiture*, placing her in the most comfortable position it allowed. Having been charged to drive slowly and carefully, the *cocher de cabriolet* mounted to his seat.

"I must not forget to ask you the name of the place where the accident happened," said M. d'Arminges, producing an ivory tablet.

"Chilworth. It is a village near Guildford. A hop-grower, Orde by name, has received him into his house, 'Ten-acre' it is called."

He scribbled down the address in full.

"And at your first convenience, monsieur, will you send a telegram to Thrupp, who is awaiting me in Rouen, at M. Grandpierre's—directing him to return to Chelsea."

"Thrupp, my patient of old," he remarked with interest. "Certainly I will," and the French address was added to the English one. "Is there anything else I can do for you ? Without doubt you are unprepared to meet the expenses you will incur by your detention here, but I will put my signature to a few cheques, which you must allow me to leave with you to be filled up at your discretion. It is very hard on you to be obliged to remain here, but I trust it will not be for long. You must not be alarmed at the bombardment, the Hôtel is situated well into the city, in the Rue de Rivoli, fifteen minutes' drive from here."

They had now reached the gate of the fortifications. The green *bois* lay behind, the "Queen City of Civilization" before them.

"The necessity of remaining here troubles me chiefly on account of the uncertainty I shall be under as to the result of the operation," she replied, wincing as the *voiture*, now passing through the Champs-Elysées, jolted over a fragment of exploded shell. "You will not, of course, be able to return?"

"I shall make the attempt. I am most

thankful that my wife and the boy are out of the place. I could not have left them here with the doubt whether I should be able to get back to them. As it is, it is awkward enough; I am sorry at having to desert my post now that my services are in such request. Only yesterday a hundred wounded were brought into the Palais de l'Industrie, and that is only one of over two hundred ambulances. But, of course, Derrick must be my first consideration, I believe it would affect my wife's reason were he to lose his, she simply idolizes him—she does not, I suppose, know anything of this?"

Glancing at her as he put the question, he was startled to see that she had swooned.

CHAPTER IX.

"My slumbers—if I slumber—are not sleep,
But a continuance of enduring thought
Which then I can resist not: in my heart
There is a vigil, and these eyes but close   ·
To look within."

Byron.

WHEN sensibility and consciousness resumed their suspended sway, Gytha found herself lying in a white-draped bed, above the wooden footboard of which appeared a dark chignon and a lamp-cast silhouette of a high, straight forehead and slightly aquiline nose. As she looked at the motionless silhouette, a mirthful laugh broke the silence. The chignon tilted backwards, and then a pair of laughing lips, and a rounded chin rose to view.

The next moment the face was turned full on her; then came an exclamation, followed by the possessor of the chignon starting to her feet, and moving round to the bedside.

"What, darling, awake and surveying your quarters?" she said, in a voice mellow and sympathetic. "And how are you feeling now—thirsty, no doubt?" and she held a glass to Gytha's parched lips.

Having drunk deeply of the refreshing draught, she looked up into the pleasant face bending over her, and asked the question,—

"Has M. d'Arminges gone?"

"Yes, dear, as soon as he had rid your arm of that pesky bullet."

"But—I don't remember anything about it. Was I unconscious?"

"Yes, dear; and I was glad you were. But don't imagine the operation was anything very dreadful; on the contrary, the bullet was very easy of extraction, for it had run up your arm and lodged on the lip of the scapula. So you don't remember coming round, and our giving you the opiate ? "

" No; the last thing I remember was being in the cab with M. d'Arminges. What time was it when he left ? "

" About four o'clock. Soon after sunset one of the carrier-pigeons returned to the cot, and they found word on her that the *Circé* had descended near Rheims. There now, you must reflect on that bit of good news whilst you eat this jelly. I think you must submit to be fed," she said, putting a spoonful of the amber jelly to Gytha's lips.

" Four o'clock, and what time is it now ? " she asked, as the spoon returned to the glass.

" Nearly one—ah, your poor arm ! " she said, as a spasm of pain contracted the pale face on the pillow. "Let me move you into a more easy position."

As the plump firm hands and muscular arms performed their work, Gytha looked up gratefully into the kind eyes that met hers.

" You are Madame—Madame—"

" I am Madame Robateau, and you are under my care until you are well and strong again," she answered, taking up glass and spoon again.

" You are very good, madame, to undertake the care of me."

" Not at all, my dear. I consider goodness is the rendering pleasantly an unpleasant service. And the service you require of me is one I take especial delight in. My mother-in-law has been pleased to declare that I am an invaluable *garde-malade*. She is bedridden, poor old soul, a martyr to rheumatism. It was on her account I remained here in Paris. She would not hear of being moved, but begged me to leave her to her fate. Leave her to her fate indeed ! I should have felt as cruel as the Northern Indians are to their sick, when they are tribing from place to place. But I did feel in a fix about Aimée—my little girl; Madame d'Arminges offered to take her with her to England, but I could not, no, I could not spare her!"

Her mellow voice became tremulous with strong emotion.

"You must indeed have felt distracted, dear madame, and, of course, will feel very anxious as long as this terrible state of things continue in Paris."

"Wa'al" (thus revealing her nationality), "I suppose I well might be, but somehow it doesn't seem in me to worry. I guess the fact is there is a hope for every fear, and I am naturally more sanguine than apprehensive. I tell the mother, to save myself from the charge of callousness, that my mind's eye is short-sighted, and can't see trouble in the distance, but this visual excuse didn't prove such a happy one as I thought, for she thinks it more than ever her duty to warn me of the dangers *she* discries in the distance—no more, dear, just this one spoonful. And now, darling, you must shut your eyes, and I my lips."

"'A hope for every fear,'" slowly repeated Gytha, "I suppose there is; though nothing but fears crowd upon me."

Madame Raboteau stooped and kissed her softly on the forehead.

"Dear child, send fears to the miller, and take heart of grace."

"But oh, madame, do you know what cause I have for my fears ? Did monsieur tell you ?"

"Yes, I know, sweet. But remember, '*Les malheurs des malheurs sont ceux qui n'arrivent jamais.*' And now try to sleep again, I am mum for the night;" and she closed her lips with an expression that barred, and double-barred them, as she took up her book and resumed her seat.

"Indeed, you must not sit up, madame, there is not the least need of it !" protested her charge.

"My dear girl, I am going to sit up, and Mark Twain—dear comical *drôle*—is going to keep me company; so you need not fear that I shall feel dull. The only fear is, that I shall laugh at his too ridiculous remarks, and disturb you!"

Obediently closing her eyes, Gytha reflected and wondered, until she fell asleep.

*　　*　　*　　*

"Three weeks! I must bear this intolerable suspense *three weeks*—unless M. d'Arminges contrives to return."

It was nearing noon, and M. d'Arminges' medical deputy had just left his English patient, having carefully redressed her wound, and informing her that she would be disabled for any exertion for at least three weeks.

"And he will return by hook or by crook. I feel sure of it!" rejoined Madame Raboteau, lifting her hazel eyes from the muslin pinafore she was darning.

"Thanks to the pigeon, we are satisfied that he is safe on his journey—or perhaps by this time he is with his brother-in-law."

"Perhaps he is performing the operation at this very minute," said Gytha, her subdued voice faltering at the thought. Then presently she suddenly turned her head sideways on the pillow, and appealed with eyes and lips to her *garde-malade*.

"Oh, madame, tell me all you know about his skill; tell me, has it ever failed?"

"Don't ask me, my love! I know very little of M. d'Arminges' doings; he seldom discusses them with any one. I questioned him once respecting his cure of a paralytic lady, a friend of mine, and I believe he thought he would satisfy my curiosity once and for ever, he went on so about cerebrum and cerebellum, their fissures, convolutions, cells by the legion and lobes with the most crack-jaw names; but when he spoke of the *legs* of the brain I sprang to my bodily ones, declaring he *was* drawing the long-bow! And would you believe it," she added, laughing, "the very next day, that child of mine—cute little chipper that she is—came to me with a doleful face and a grievance. She had laid open her doll's head; and the grievance was that, 'they hadn't put any legs or funny things inside!' She must have been in the room when monsieur made his statements, and been more impressed with them than I was."

"And made her doll the subject for anatomy," said Gytha, smiling. "What a practical little woman she must be! I am afraid she must have rued having made such a sacrifice to science."

"Yes, she did at first; but, when I told monsieur of her vain researches, he laughed, and straightway set himself to repair the mischief. His operation was perfectly successful; and Aimée was as proud as Punch to tell her little friends that M. d'Arminges had cured 'Mamzelle

Lorinne's' head. But before 'Mamzelle Lorinne' went the way of all dolls, she rejoiced in a whole string of aliases, for she was renamed again and again after those of the fair sex on whom monsieur had wrought his most wonderful cures. The alias under which she became defunct was *L'alouette,* after a favourite songstress, who, to the deploration of the operatic world, unaccountedly lost the power of speech, or as the *Figaro* had it, 'The sweet tongue, that had spell-bound so many, was itself spell-bound;' which spell was broken by monsieur, who trepanned her skull, and removed the cause of dumbness. Young O'Rorke, who was here visiting his sister at the time, scribbled a parody on it, in one of Aimée's rhyme-books :—

> "Who cured *L'alouette?*
> 'I,' said the Frenchman,
> 'With my bright trepan,
> I cured L'alouette.'

"But I am afraid I am making your

head ache with my chatter," she said, seeing that her listener's brows were drawn as with pain.

" No, indeed, madame; when I am not listening to you, I am listening to my thoughts, and they make my heart ache."

" My dear child, you really must not give way to such misgivings! What has become of the 'grit' that carried you flying over the Prussians' heads? It was too bad of them to fire at the balloon; but, of course, they couldn't see you were a petticoated blockade-flyer, or I guess they would have desisted. Now, if, like Duruof, you had sent down *your* cartes-de-visite, it would have been something to the purpose!"

" I am afraid the 'something' would have ended in smoke," said Gytha, attempting a responsive lightness.

" Oh, I must not forget to tell you, M. d'Arminges had your balloon taken to M. Flaud's manufactory to be repaired, and he asked me to suggest to you the advisability—in case of your being obliged to return by balloon—of making the attempt by night."

"It was very kind of him to consider me. Certainly it would be wise to avoid the danger of being seen."

CHAPTER X.

" But day doth daily draw my sorrows longer,
  And night doth nightly make grief's strength seom
    stronger."

Shakspere

" I WISH Susanne would curl my hair like *maman* does. They will be straight before ' mamzelle ' sees me, I'm sure they will ! " lamented a little girl, who was standing on tiptoe before a pier-glass, craning her plump little neck in order the better to view the loose raven curls falling down her back.

The sound of a turning handle made her move away from the glass as quickly and self-conscious as if her years had been trebled ; and a shy look stole from her

dark eyes as the door opened, admitting
" mamzelle," closely followed by *maman.*

" Why, Aimée, am I more formidable
up than abed, that you don't come and
kiss me ? " asked the former, as she took
the *fauteuil* Madame Raboteau wheeled for
her before an American stove.

" Run and place a footstool for mademoiselle."

Aimée darted towards the article in
request, and seizing it by one of its ears,
dragged it to the invalid's feet ; and, as
she adjusted it, looked up with returning
confidence into the pale face she had been
accustomed to see mated to a pillow.

Gytha drew the child to her with her
free arm, and pressed a kiss upon the lips
that matched in hue the bright cherry
ribbon that tied back the dubious curls.

" Where are Uncle Tom, Henrietta, and
Captain Jinks ? Won't you introduce
them to me ? " she requested, and in a
minute her lap was an assembly-room for

a maimed darkie in striped habiliments the worse for wear ; a comparatively sound-limbed, freshly-attired Jack Tar; and a dainty *Parisienne,* with a model bonnet perched on her golden chignon.

By the time they were all introduced Aimée's tongue was its usual tripping self.

" Yes, isn't she *élégant !* " she exclaimed admiringly, as Gytha praised the appearance of the fashionable damsel. " I used to wash her face in milk every morning, but now I can't have any. *Maman* says it is wasteful; we want every drop to drink. *Maman,*" she called to madame, who had turned her face aside to hide an expression that hovered between vexation and amusement. " *Maman,* when I was out this morning with Susanne, I saw a little girl give her doll—such a beautiful doll, to that big statue with the funny name—Stras—Strasbourg—and the people cheered her, and called her ' *Une petite patriote.'*   May I give Henrietta, and be called '*Une petite patriote,*' too, *chère maman ?*"

"What, would you sacrifice poor Henrietta ?" said Gytha.

"Oh, she would like it! Shall I put her on her pink silk or her blue muslin dress, *maman*, or do you think she looks best in this ?" doubtfully eyeing the silver-grey costume.

"We will decide that another time, *ma mie*," answered Madame Raboteau, using the endearment her husband had been wont to apply to his little daughter.

"And *maman*, when we were coming back through the Place de la Concorde, we met such a big crowd, and a lot of soldiers, and some of them had pieces of cardboard in front of them with writing; Susanne said it was to tell all good citizens to spit on them, but I said it could not be that, because it is very rude to spit. But she said they had been very *méchant*, and ran away when they were wanted to fight. I asked her where they were taking them, but before she could tell me, a great rough woman turned round and told her not to tell me; and she pinched my cheek. Oh, her hands did smell so of garlic! But where were they taking them, *maman?*"

"How can I tell you, my child, I did not see them," answered her mother lightly. But her face turned pale, for she knew full well the poor fellows were going to be shot. And seeing her sudden pallor, Gytha guessed as much.

"Now, mademoiselle, if you will excuse me, and you, Aimée, promise not to be tiresome, I will go to *bonne maman*," said Madame Raboteau, taking up her work-basket.

"I can answer for Aimée," said Gytha, her white fingers toying with the raven curls, to the blended apprehension and complacence of that little damsel.

Before long, observing certain wistful

glances her little companion cast towards the window, Gytha proposed that they should go hither and look out.

Clapping her hands in delighted acquiescence, Aimée ran and arranged the cushions of a lounging-chair facing the window ; and, having satisfied herself that " mamzelle " was comfortable, she perched herself on another.

There was plenty to see and talk about, for the window overlooked the Tuileries Gardens, now exhibiting all the characteristics of an artillery camp ; huge guns, uniform tents, pickets of horses, and busy knots of soldiers.

" I wish I could go in the gardens and play again," said Aimée, her blithe voice taking a rueful accent. " I have no one to play with now, not even Derry ; I did cry so, when he went away with Madame d'Arminges."

" Derry," repeated Gytha, with eager interest.

"That isn't his proper name, it's Derrick, really. And his uncle, who is called Derrick too, came here last Christmas. I did love him dearly, *dearly!* He took me and Derry to such lots of pantomimes, and he was always buying us *jouets* and *bonbons*, and last birthday he sent me a locket, a gold one with a real diamond in it. Oh, it's such a beauty! And—wasn't it comical, mamzelle?—we didn't know for a long time that it opened, till one day when I was looking at it, it flew right open, and there was Uncle Derrick looking out! He isn't my uncle really, you know, but he told me to call him so. *Maman* has it put away, but I will run and ask her to let me show it to you;" and she was starting off with that intention, when "mamzelle" called after her in a strange, sharp voice,—

"No, no, Aimée; I could not bear to look at it now!"

"Oh, mamzelle, are you going to faint? Shall I call maman?" said the child, looking with great concern at the pale, pained face of the *malade.*

" No, dear, come and sit down again. I shall be better presently."

Aimée returned reluctantly to her seat, and, with disappointed pout, fixed her eyes on the scene below.

Leaning back in her chair, Gytha closed her eyes, to give rein to anxious wonder concerning the giver of that locket. If M. d'Arminges could but return, and end this restless suspense that swayed her thoughts by day and her dreams by night! Only the previous night he had appeared in her dream as one who " sees more devils than vast hell can hold."

" Oh, look, mamzelle, what a crowd! They are mobbing such a funny little man. Hark! they are shouting '*Espion!*'"

Being thus called on by her little friend, Gytha looked out on the excited rabble, the attraction of which was an undersized man in Zouave uniform, who was wedged between two stolid *agents de police.*

The instant her glance fell on his flat bald head, she started to her feet, and to Aimée's amazement threw open the window, and stepping out on the balcony, frantically waved her handkerchief, crying the while, "Thrupp! Thrupp!! Thrupp!!!"

Her gesticulation and outcry quickly effected a general halt. The person whom she addressed looked up joyfully, the *agents de police* suspiciously, and the crowd expectantly.

"*Il n'est pas un espion; il est mon serviteur!*" she cried excitedly.

"Tak' care, miss! Dinna ye trouble yoursel'; I'se be a' richt," shrilly shouted Thrupp, his guarded little person wriggling with alarm, lest his excited advocate should in her eagerness overbalance herself over the low balcony.

She was just about to again address his

dubious-looking custodians, when her glance fell on a horseman, who had drawn rein on the outskirts of the mob, and to her joy she recognized the chasseur officer who had befriended her on the frontier.

Saluting her as their eyes met, he dismounted, gave his horse in charge of a soldier, and bidding the *agents* await his return, entered the hotel. His martial figure had no sooner disappeared within the vestibule than the crowd also lost sight of the crimson-robed one that had leant over the balcony. And again raising the cry, *'Espion! Espion!'* they pressed around the suspected one and his guards, who had as much as they could do to keep their ground. They were beginning to cast impatient glances towards the hotel entrance, when the officer reappeared and commanded them to advance, and the mob to fall back, which latter command was set at nought, greatly to the hindrance of the guards. But at length captive and captors reached the steps of the hotel. The chasseur addressed a few words to the officers of the peace in a language unintelligible to Thrupp, but which proved effectual in delivering the Scotchman from their custody into that of a sleek-looking *garçon*, who, eyeing him with disfavour, conducted him up the stairs to a certain door and admitted him into an elegant saloon. And there stood Gytha, expectantly and hopefully, yet with a look of dread in her eyes.

"Oh, Thrupp, what brings you here? Thank heaven you're safe! What horrible creatures to mob you like that!"

"What I hae dune to deserve it, I dinna ken," said he. Then, looking down on his strange garments, he added, "Maybe it is the gear, but an I could mak' shift wi' it, I dinna see why that riff-raff couldna. They micht hae seen it was a quiet eneugh body in itsel', but it's sma' gumption these puir folks are blessed wi'. It was lucky ye saw me, miss, for I doobt I wad e'er hae found ye. I lost my cap, an' the bit of paper wi' the name o' this house, when I was swimming up the river!"

"Swimming up the river! Was that how you managed to get in?"

"Aye, last night."

"But have you seen M. d'Arminges—where do you come from?"

"Frae the bedside o' that ailing gentleman."

Gytha's heart leapt within her.

"How is he?" she asked in a tense undertone.

"Longing to know how it fares wi' yoursel'. An' that is but puirly, I fear," he said, regarding her sadly, "the flesh frae your banes, an' the blume frae your cheek."

But even as he regarded her, the pale face bloomed anew, with sudden rush of joyful emotion, a lovely rose-glow that passed away all too quickly ; but the paleness it left was not as the paleness it had found. It was as different as ice from snow.

"He knows then—his reason is saved ?" she said, her voice tremulous with joy over that long-prayed-for salvation.

" Aye, as much as there was o't ! He began to mend as sune as the wee bit o' bane was raised frae his brain. So Dr. d'Arminges told me. I didna get there till the next day."

"But how was it you went to Chilworth ? Did he not telegraph to you ?"

" Telling me how ye were obleeged to bide here, and bidding me go back to Chelsea. Aye, I got it, but misteuk Chelsea for Chilworth, an' started offhand, an' never found oot what a fule I had been till I got there ! When I told the doctor I was minded to get away to ye somehow, an' how I thoucht to win by the blockade, he said, ' Bide a day or two an' we will make the attempt together.'   But when we got to London, and went to see his wife and boy, he found the puir bairn very ill, an' like to die in fact.   An' so he cudna leave him."

" No, of course he could not ; I do hope he may be able to save him !   How thankful he must feel that he is not here, in ignorance of his danger.   And so you came on alone, and made the attempt.   It was very, very kind of you to face so much danger, to say nothing of the coldness and wretchedness of it ! "

" Hoot-toot, that was naething !   An' I had water outside the body o' me, I had whuskey inside.   The warst o' it was, I had to leave maist o' my clothing behind me, an' when I gat here there was naething for me but these queer clothes that some sodgers took off a puir chap who had been shot down.   It was kin' o' them, but I wad never hae put leg into his red breeks an I had ken'd they wad bring that crowd o' folks aboot me, like a lot o' rampagious cattle."

"They took you for a spy," said Gytha, who could scarcely repress a smile at the figure he cut in the wide red "breeks" and jaunty cutaway jacket, displaying linen that was not of the cleanest.

"A spy! The deil take them for a pack o' fules!" he exclaimed, shaking his lithe little body. Then as he met Aimée's wondering gaze, his irritated expression gave place to a smile : "Weel, my dainty dove, an' will ye tell me the name o' ye?"

"Mademoiselle Aimée Raboteau," she announced with pretty dignity. Then she condescended to ·inquire confidentially, "Monsieur Thrupp, how old are you?"

"My goodness! dinna 'Moosoo' me, little leddy! Hoo old am I? Weel, I guess I count six years to your one. An' noo I hae told ye, will ye gie me a kiss frae those bonny lips?" he asked, going down on his knees that she might the easier grant the boon. But Aimée shrunk from him in undisguised aversion, her distended eyes fixed on his bald, flat head, beneath whose membraneous surface the convoluted brain could be seen distinctly throbbing.

" Will-a-wa, I forget what a scarecrow I am ! " he sharply exclaimed, springing to his feet. " Maybe, it was the head o' me, an' nae the breeks, that made them abuse me just noo. Pugh, I wad rather lack the shell nor the kernel ! " he concluded, recovering his usual cheerful alacrity.

" Thrupp ! You have had breakfast ? " said Gytha, the thought having suddenly struck her, that perhaps he had not.

" Ne'er a bit ! An' I had my cap I wad hold it to ye for a few coppers—but an' I had my cap I shouldna need them ; for I tucked awa' a few gold coins in the lining o't."

" Oh, Thrupp, and I have been so

thoughtlessly detaining you here !" she regretfully exclaimed, putting her hand to her pocket, forgetful that it was her dressing-gown she wore. " Run, dear," she said, turning to Aimée, " and ask *maman* to give you my purse."

" An' when I hae had bit an' sop, I will gae an' see aboot the puir *Serena*, for it is hersel' we will be wanting as sune as ye are hale again."

" She has already been repaired, thanks to M. d'Arminges; and now I have you to manage her, I shall be able to return very soon," she replied, with animation.

"I maunna forget, miss, Maister O'Rorke told me to gie ye his maist kind regards, an' to say as how glad he will be to see ye again."

" You saw him, then ?" she asked, fingering the ribbon *ruche* that adorned the front of her gown.

" Aye, jist afore I come awa'. He maun

hae gude blude in him, an I am a judge o' looks !" he averred.

"Does he suffer much?" she said, raising her eyes from the *ruche* and meeting his with an anxious expression.

"It is the back o' him that pains maist, it is sairly sprained, the doctor told me, though he made light o' it himsel'. He is very vexed aboot your arm, an' sae was the auld leddy. She bid me say she wad hae a room ready for ye, an ye wad like to return an' bide a time wi' her. An' that burly son o' hers wha was standing. by, told me to min' an' gie ye the message, word for word; an' moreover to be sure an' sen' them word as sune as e'er we get out o' Paris."

At this point Aimée returned, accompanied by her mother. The cordial smile the latter bestowed on Gytha's odd-looking visitor, showed that Aimée must have been giving her some account of "Monsieur Thrupp."

She insisted on his breakfasting there and then. Consequently in a short space of time, hot rolls, grilled ham and steaming coffee, were aromatizing the atmosphere, and at Madame Raboteau's invitation, Krupp seated himself with alacrity before the plenteous repast.

"This is na horse, an' na donkey, but a cut frae the ham o' as plump a piggy as e'er grunted!" was his inward comment, as his sharp white teeth and a piece of the delicately cooked slice came into contact.

Thanks to Madame Raboteau's forethought, before he left the Hôtel Wagram he doffed the Zouave uniform and donned a spare suit of one of the *garçons*.

CHAPTER XI.

"O love, my love! if I no more should see
Thyself, nor on the earth the shadow of thee,
Nor image of thine eyes in any spring,—
How then should sound upon Life's darkening slope,
The ground-whirl of the perished leaves of Hope,
The wind of Death's imperishable wing?"

D. G. Rossetti.

"I WOULD that son of Anak would give me a little of his company. He would probably bore me; but my own company more than bores—it palls on me!"

At this point in his self-communion Derrick O'Rorke impatiently jerked himself, which caused acute pain. He then cautiously shifted himself into a different position, and from studying the pattern of the chintz curtain on his right hand fell to studying that on his left.

"I feel sure Thrupp has won his way in somehow, or he would have shown up again by this time. Did I but know how he found her! What if he found her—*dead*." A thin vein-marked hand was pressed to the clammy brow that harboured this grim fear. "I am convinced D'Arminges was more anxious about her than he cared to let me see. I hope, for her sake, he will be for getting back to Paris, now that Derry has turned the corner. But of course Fan will do her very utmost to prevent him," and the thin hand wandered over the counterpane, to meet with the sought-for letter. Turning to the second page, the clinic reperused it.

"I am so thankful to be able to say that darling Derry is out of danger; but I am no sooner relieved from that anxiety than I have another, Émile says he *must* return to Paris! But rather than let him go, I will take something to make me dreadfully ill. I never felt so grateful to any one as I do to Miss Keppel, though it was for the big Derry, and not for the little one, she faced so many dangers. Fancy, Emile told me that if that horrid bullet had swerved but half an inch it would have severed the main artery, and she would have bled to death! I do hope there is no fear as yet of her not having sufficient and proper nourishment. How I wish we could hear how she is going on! That poor little oddity! I wonder if his aquatic scheme succeeded. I am truly thankful Émile did not go with him, and am *determined* he shall not follow him. The very thought distracts me. If only this wretched, wretched siege could have been avoided." "If only"—groaned O'Rorke, flinging hand and letter at arm's length from him, and staring hard into vacancy,—"She would never have made that perilous venture—she would not now be enduring Heaven knows what, in that accursed place! 'Sufficient and proper nourishment,' surely she does not lack that? The doubt will, choke me every time I swallow food!" He turned his face to the pillow and breathed a prayer— insomuch that it was the most sincere desire that had ever wrung his soul— for the welfare of her who was to his heart as emotion, to his mind as conscience.

Again reverting to the letter, he went on with its perusal : "I have this morning received a letter from Aunt Kate, dated the 2nd instant, Buffalo, stating that the *Shannon* would set sail for home in a few days. They intend putting in at Greenwich, in order to see me and yourself. But probably, sir, you have been already informed of their movements by your *fiancée*, for convinced of the beneficial effects of a *billet-doux*, I induced Émile to leave directions at the Temple, that all foreign letters should be forwarded to you." "I would as soon the *Shannon* was *not* going to put in at Greenwich," he muttered; "aunt will be swooping down on me for a certainty, and probably Eileen. Well, it behoves me to be grateful for the certainty, and—delighted at the probability ! " an unpleasant humour gleamed from the deep-set eyes fixed on the corkscrew flourish—worthy of Charles Lamb's pen—at the close of the lengthy letter. The next minute a sound in the direction of the door attracted his eyes thither, to behold the huge figure of Mark Orde filling the way.

"How   is   this—where   is   Widow Tribble ? " he queried, looking round the room as he closed the door behind him.

" I observed that sleep weighed on her eyelids, so implored her to seek her pillow; whether she has succeeded in finding it, I cannot tell you," replied O'Rorke, eyeing his visitor with languid interest as he came round to the bedside.

Then perceiving he held a sheet of orange-coloured paper in his hand, he asked quickly, " What's that—news ? "

" Yes, and good news, I rejoice to say," replied Orde, thrusting the telegram into the other's open hand.

" Left Paris with Thrupp, 12.30. a.m. Descended here"—a glance at the heading showed " here," to be Villequier —" safely 2.25. Start for Dieppe immediately. Hope to reach Chilworth this evening."

" By the saints ! That gives the *quietus* to our anxiety !" exclaimed O'Rorke, in a voice unsteady with excess of feeling, as was also the hand holding the swift-sped message that had changed the knell in his heart to a joy-bell. " No more harrowing doubts. She is in the land of the living, and the land of plenty, thank Heaven ! "

" She has been guarded from many dangers. I have been afraid all along that she would be obliged to have recourse to that risky balloon," rejoined Orde, his stentorian voice subdued.

"That manikin of hers deserves a medal for his pluck! We owe it to him that she is out of Paris. She cannot be equal to the management of the *Serena.*"

" To think of a delicate woman and a 'manikin' braving such perils, whilst these strong limbs of mine were lumbering my bed!" exclaimed Orde, with strong self-disgust.

"My dear fellow, they would have lumbered her car more than they did your bed! You need not begrudge them their tonicity," said O'Rorke dryly. " 'Hope to reach Chilworth this evening,'" he repeated, as though by utterance to enhance the pleasure of scanning the delightful words.

"I hope she is not overtaxing her strength. I shall start for Newhaven to meet her by the 2.50 train," said the other, seating himself sideways on the edge of the bed.

" My good giant, you'll capsize me ! " irritably warned the clinic.

" How's that ! Lost weight in the night ? " said the ' giant ' good-humouredly, as he stood up. " By-the-bye, what sort of a night did you have ? "

" Tolerably good," was the mendacious answer, " I shall get Cobhold to sanction my getting up on the strength of it."

" Get up, man ! Why I thought it was only yesterday he said you would have to lie on your back for at least a week longer ! "

" Confound my back ! It's abominable being bed-ridden in this fashion."

" You may be thankful you are not *grave*-ridden," said Orde seriously.

" Faith ! that confinement would be worse than this ! I hope I may be brimful of days before the All-dreaded Sheriff does indeed serve a capias on me. But an inkling gleamed on me just now, from a remark of Widow Tribble, that it was my reason that was in danger. Was it so?"

"You were near, dear friend, losing that Pearl of Great Price," was the grave reply.

"Egad, and so it was to secure the pearl in its setting, that D'Arminges tinkered my brain-pan!"

"Yes, and remember it was mercifully preserved to you, to cherish as a divine illumination unto the path of wisdom. See that no breath of the devil tarnish it. See that its light guides you to higher than worldly distinctions. Alas! how many go down into hell, because it is their chief desire, their grand aim, to rise in this world."

In mute astonishment, O'Rorke looked up at the stern-browed, fervid-eyed admonisher towering at his side, who, turning abruptly on his heel, moved towards the fireplace.

"Why, what fiery fanatic have we here?" mentally exclaimed the invalid, as he watched Orde bend his broad back and throw fresh logs on the glowing pile heaped high on the hearth-stone. " The fire's well enough in all conscience. Possibly he sees a visionary heretic among the flames, and feels he must add a faggot or two," he thought on, with a whimsical smile.

But the " fanatic" turning round and coming back to the bed, O'Rorke saw that the glowing fervency had faded from the heavily-browed eyes, leaving in them a disturbed expression, instead of their usual quietude.

" I have some matters I must look to before starting," he said, coming to a halt at the foot of the bed. " I will tell mother you are alone."

. " I beg you will not trouble her; I am all right," O'Rorke assured him.

" I shall look in again before I leave," said Orde, looking back as he reached the door.

" Well, he is a queer one, now as cool as a cucumber, and now as hot as a cayenne-pod! But I wouldn't mind being in his shoes for the rest of the day— provided they are not hobnailed!" added the 'knight templar' as he listened to the other's retreating footsteps. "'Go to Newhaven to meet her.' Lucky dog that he can! He will see the packet nearing and nearing—he will see her coming over the gangway, and he will step forward and take her hand in his, where I am sure it will be lost! Then he will conduct her to the train, and settle her in a cosy corner, and himself in another cosy corner. And I shall be lying here—" he groaned in spirit, then his national buoyancy asserting itself, he went on gaily with his prospective reverie. "But I shall see that door"—regarding its stolid oaken face—"slowly open, and lo! on the threshold the Witch will stand! And she will look—she will look as she did when she turned round from her bread-and-butter cutting. Alack, *I* shan't be able to step forward and meet her, or make any obeisance—unless I pull my forelock! But no, I cannot even do that, they have shaven and shorn me so. Confound it!" putting his hand up to his closely clipped head. "I am glad the bandages are off; I shall look a little less like a worsted house-breaker. Then—then she will come and shake my hand, and my heart to boot! What will her first words be? One seems to see her words as much as hear them, they curve her lips into such witchery. I wish these words were in her own writing." And his eyes again rested on the orange-coloured paper, so flimsy in itself, so weighty in its import. "I wish

I could induce her to give up this aërial jaunting. She will certainly never let me ' summer high in heaven ' again."

The entrance of his mild, placid-looking nurse put an end to his ruminations.

CHAPTER XII.

"Joy, so true and tender,
Dare you not abide?
Will you spread your pinions,
Must you leave our side?
Adelaide A. Procter.

THE day was older by ten hours, and the clinic was directing expectant glances towards the door, whose stolid face was now cheerily expressive by reason of playing gleams of firelight. An occasional crackle from the burning logs, together with the clink, clink, of Widow Tribble's knitting-needles, alone broke the silence.

At last his alert ears detected the tap, tap of heels on the stone passage without. Nearer and nearer they came. There was a pause, then the sound of a lifting latch. The door opened slowly, and lo! there stood—the Quakeress! Then as her tall, erect figure stepped forward, his peering eyes fell on one of supple slightness—one whom he had last seen standing motionless in the down-whirling car. His eager vigilance gave place to contentment, as the Witch followed her conductress into the room, and the full blazes of firelight illumined her features, even to the revelation of the little black mole on her chin.

"Praise be to Him who hath preserved ye to this joyful meeting," said Mrs. Orde, with low and solemn voice.

"Amen," reverently rejoined a voice, whose soft clearness the invalid so well remembered. Then Gytha came quickly forward, and he saw "the sweet splendour of her smile" shining from her dark eyes, and a hand, that seemed a fair gleaming incarnation of voice and smile, met his outstretched palm.

"I hoped to find you further on the road to recovery, Mr. O'Rorke," she said.

"Faith, Miss Keppel, you might well expect it, but I am travelling by such absurdly easy stages! I feel confident I should get on faster if I took to my legs, instead of remaining in this slow-coach; but its conductor, one Christopher Cobhold, won't hear of it."

"I hope you are not an unruly fare," she responded, as she took the chintz-covered chair Mrs. Orde had drawn to the bed-side before she went over to the fire-place, where she now stood in conference with Widow Tribble, respecting the invalid's evening meal.

"Apropos of the topic yonder," began the invalid, "I have had some awful misgivings that you were lacking delicacies, while I have been overwhelmed with them," looking at her as he spoke, he was shocked to see how sharpened were the delicate outlines of her features.

"Indeed I have not! I have lacked neither delicacies nor care. A sister could not have been more kind to me than Madame Raboteau has been. She sent her regards to you, and best wishes for your speedy recovery. And Aimée charged me to tell you to be sure. and come again next Christmas."

"Poor little mortal, I fear Christmas will bring her but few pleasures! I wish she and her mother were well out of Paris. I had a letter from my sister this morning, saying that Derry is out of danger, and that D'Arminges insists on returning to Paris."

"Oh, I hope not! That would indeed mar her joy at her son's recovery."

"Just so. I sent a telegram to him this afternoon, begging him not to give Fan yet further cause for anxiety," he rejoined with a twinge of consciousness at the thought that his sister's anxiety *had* been but a secondary consideration.

" Has the distress made much headway there as yet ? "

" Yes, among the lower classes it has," she answered sadly. " The poor people look half starved already, but for all that they protest against capitulation."

" A patriotic starveling is utterly beyond my comprehension," he said, with an incautious shrug that made him wince. Seeing she noted his involuntary expression of pain, he went on quickly, " Unpalatable as humble pie is, I should for my own part infinitely prefer eating it, to starving. So Thrupp contrived to *swim* the blockade ? "

" That he did ! " she said, smiling, and added an amusing account of his appearance and adventures.

" Fancy that natty little precisian having to wander about in that outlandish gear ! " he laughed, " but I'll be bound he felt fully recompensed for passing through such an ordeal, when he piloted you in triumph over the heads of the Prussians. I am afraid you must have found the journey very trying," he added solicitously, his eyes on her sling-supported arm.

"Not at all. Thrupp saw to everything. All I had to do was to 'sit and be blowed along,' as Captain Potter expressed it." A smile flitted across O'Rorke's lips.

"And the descent—I hope he effected an easy one. Your poor arm could ill encounter any jolting."

As she saw and heard the tenderness of look and voice, a sweet hope stole into her heart, there to be infolded in her love's embrace.

"He was most careful. The *Serena* came down as gently as a dove," she assured him, a soft warm rose-flush tinting her pale cheek the while.

"I am very glad to hear that. I lay awake during the time of your perilous journey, all unwitting what cause I had for keeping vigil."

Her eyes drooped before his impulsive glance, and fell to tracing the veins of the wasted hand lying on the coverlet.

"It seems like a blessed dream, your sitting there! How I have longed to thank you for all you have hazarded and undergone on my account. And now I can find no words—"

"Thanks! Whatever thanks are due to me, I owe you twofold! But I cannot thank, for wanting to censure you; nor censure, for wanting to thank you. How could you have taken that rash leap!"

"Then I hope the one desire will swallow the other, and finally swallow itself, like a pantomimic marvel. But, seriously, I hold myself chargeable with the whole catastrophe. Had I used more persuasion and less force with that luckless guide-rope, the poor *Serena* might not have given up the ghost so precipitately."

" How horrible it was ! " she said, a sudden pallor, the ghost of her past horror, stealing over her face.

" You will laugh at me when I tell you I imagined there were numbers of open graves gaping beneath us, which I have since ascertained were veritably—*hopbins !* "

" Open graves—what an awful delusion ! " she said, the tremor in her voice telling him that the ludicrousness of his supposition was lost in its all but tragic congruity.

" How intensely she feels—how intensely she could love ! Perhaps some happy fellow could tell me she *does* love ! And I have been lying here bewailing my want of liberty to woo, when the chances are I should have failed to win ! " he thought, as he watched the fascinating revelations of the fitful firelight—revelations of a pale fair face, from whence looked eyes, glorious with intelligence and feeling. Suddenly a wan light, proceeding from the other end of the room, drew his attention to the fact that Mrs. Orde had lighted a candle, to whose dim flame her snowy cap was the next minute brought in close proximity, in her endeavours to read the label on one of those dose-marked bottles so familiar to his eyes. At last she raised her head and looked across the room.

" Wilt thou come here and read these directions, Gytha Keppel," she requested, " mine eyes fail me by candlelight."

Followed by O'Rorke's gaze, Gytha moved away to her side, and read the minute directions, her voice reaching O'Rorke in a vague murmur.

As she returned and tendered him the potion-glass, he remembered how the lady-witch was want to administer

"— liquors clear and sweet, whose healthful might
Could medicine the sick soul to happy sleep."

But, alas! he found the dark-coloured mixture anything but " clear and sweet."

" Mrs. Orde tells me I must say good-night now," she said, placing the promptly emptied glass on a small table close by, and holding out her hand.

As he held it in his, he expressed a hope that a restful night would wait on the fatiguing day she had spent.

CHAPTER XIII.

Derrick O'Rorke to Henry Harwood, London.

Chilworth, October 22nd, 1870.

"Dear Hal,—But that my back has been flatly opposed to any such proceeding, I should have long since notified the arrival of the news-laden argosy so humanely despatched by you to your 'forlorn and *balloon*-wrecked brother.'

" You speak very modestly of your legal *début*, but in a few lines I yesterday received from Bolgor, he announced that General Commendation has espoused your Maiden Speech. May a succession of promising little briefs be the issue thereof !

I would you could have given me better accounts of poor little Lagarde. I have been wondering if he were still excitedly arguing himself into coughing fits. I could not but fear the last time I saw him, that there was more likelihood of his putting on angelic, than legal vesture.

"On your apprising me that it was Madame Fanchon who had acquainted you with my adventures and misadventures, I was prepared to find you had imbibed exaggerated notions of them. As to my having been all but *impaled on a hop-pole*, I am not in a position to refute; but as to being *dragged miles out to sea by the balloon*, that is an assertion which requires to be curtailed by *miles*; half a cable's length was the extent of its towage, thanks to the smacksman who came to my aid. But for him, I fear it would have gone hard with Miss Keppel—as she is known to you —the Witch of Atlas, as she is known to me. Yes, *mon gaillard*, the vision seen by me, flouted by you, is at last verified beyond doubt. Her own lips have confirmed that she was on that identical mountain that self-same eve ; but whether she vanished within leafy abode of Hamadryad, or liquid bower of Oread, I have not yet discovered. I confess I was not a little surprised at her reappearance on the North Sea, until I remembered how she would sometimes ascend

> '— to those streams of upper air,
> Which whirl the earth in its diurnal round.'

"With regard to her untimely descent, I could only conclude that one of those bearded braves of the sidereal world had sighted her eyes from afar, and under the delusion they were fair acquaintances, had straightway darted to greet them, inadvertently piercing her silken sphere in his precipitancy.

"'What bosh!' I hear you exclaim. But, my dear fellow, have you not found at times, when your 'bosom's lord sits lightly in his throne,' his Fool is quick to take advantage, and you will comprehend how lightly sits mine, when I tell you Miss Keppel is no longer amidst the perils and privations of Paris, but safe in this peaceful vale—this peaceful dwelling ! She left the poor Queen City with Pate-in-Peril— as you call him—12.30 on the 19th instant, descending at Villequier 2.25, and arrived here at sundown,—

" The foregoing hyphen represents an interruption in the burly form of Mark Orde. His first deed—its evil odour even now offendeth my olfactory sense—was to thrust his great boots amongst the burning logs, thereby sending one flying unto the sheepskin hearthrug. His next, to send a boxful of bolus pills rolling in every direction over the floor. Whilst he was on all-fours hunting after them, he imparted to me that he was about to take Miss Keppel to the Surrey Hills, to view the prospect therefrom. As soon as he had left the room,

I took the precaution to throw the laboriously-recovered pills behind the fire; returning to my seat just in time to see the Witch and him leave the house together. As I watched his unwieldy ponderosity, I could not but think of the elephant, who was drawn with other 'gaunt and sanguine beasts,' within the imparadising presence of the Witch.

"You must wonder how much longer I am going to prick " *Æyer*," but somehow I don't seem to wax strong, despite unlimited draughts of hop-bitters—the brewage of my worthy hostess—which heretofore I have infinitely preferred to those of Doctor Cobbold; but the elephant this morning turned the tide of my predilection, by expatiating on insects twain, that spoileth the tender vine, viz. the hop-flea and louse! Confound the fellow! How shall I ever again enjoy my once favourite glass of B.B.B.? I wish, at your earliest convenience, you would send me vols. VII. and

XI. of Brougham's Works, and if you sandwich "Shelley" between them, shall be glad, for I am in a literary Sahara— excepting religious treatises. The most attractive I could find among the lot Orde brought me, was "Tupper's Philosophy," on which I have been solely existing. I will quote a line from his "Friendship,"

'Those hours are not lost that are spent in cementing affection,'

as a hint for you to soon convert ink to that adhesive purpose, and write to your sincere friend,

"DERRICK O'RORKE."

MADAME D'ARMINGES to DERRICK O'RORKE, Chilworth.

Grosvenor Square, October 25th, 1870.

"MY VERY DEAR BROTHER,—To-day has been a most wretched, distressing one. Not only has it brought the separation I have so dreaded and tried to prevent, but trouble from a quarter whence we—especially you—have been looking only for pleasure. I don't know how to write what will so pain and outrage your feelings, but I have promised aunt to do so. I found her and uncle here, on my return from Dover—I would go that far with my dear Émile. I thought aunt looked very pale and worried, but attributed it to concern on your behalf, when I heard that Mrs. Cumberland had already acquainted them with your accident. You may imagine my surprise when on my inquiring for Eileen, aunt burst into tears. My first fear was that she was dead, but aunt's coloured dress reassured me on that point. Then uncle thundered out a story that pained me beyond words, knowing how it would affect you.

"I don't know whether you have ever heard that when they had made arrangements for their voyage to America, uncle's old captain, Baines, was taken ill. So a friend of uncle, Captain Wilmott—who on the death of his father a short time before, had retired from the navy—offered to take command of the *Shannon*. During the outward voyage, aunt noticed that he and Eileen seemed to find great pleasure in each others company; and asked the latter if she had informed him of her engagement to you. Her answer was, 'Oh yes, don't alarm yourself, you dear old fidget, we are only having a little flirtation.' But at length Captain Wilmott's attentions became so marked, that uncle requested him to discontinue them, adding, that he should not have permitted such, had Eileen been free to accept them. And wound up by saying that perhaps the most satisfactory course would be for Captain Wilmott to resign his post. To which he replied, that he would do so as soon as uncle had engaged another to fill it. The *Shannon* was then making for Buffalo.

On arriving there, uncle engaged private

apartments, thinking that if they went to a hotel, Captain Wilmott might also take up his quarters there. But his precaution was of no avail, for on the following morning, while he and aunt were waiting breakfast for Eileen, there arrived a note from her, saying she had early that morning been married to Captain Wilmott, at St. Paul's, and that they were then staying at the Delaware Hotel, where she hoped they would come and see her before she and her husband started for St. Louis. This uncle decidedly refused to do, and it was some time before he would assent to aunt going. When she at length reached the hotel, it was to find they had just left for the station, where she at once drove, reaching the platform just as the train was on the move. But as it was gliding by, Eileen looked from one of the windows and kissed her hand.

Her heartlessness deserves nothing more or less than contempt, and that I hope

will with you outweigh all other feelings.
I wish I could go to you instead of writing;
but they tell me darling Derry almost
broke his heart this morning, when he
found I had left him.

I have not yet said, dear, how glad I
was to see by your letter yesterday, that
you are so much better. I do hope you
will not let this trouble prey on your
mind, but fear you will have too many
opportunities of doing so. I wish Miss
Keppel had been able to prolong her visit.
I must manage to run up to Chelsea and
see her before she leaves England.

I will write to you again as soon as I
receive a telegram from Émile. I scarcely
know what to hope respecting his pass-
port. I have implored him, in case he
should fail to obtain one, not to risk his
life by attempting Thrupp's, or any other
dangerous expedient, but he would not
give me his promise. I do wish arith-
mancy could divine when this dreadful siege

will end. I shall certainly never laugh
at its divining power again, since its
prophecy of this being a year of disaster
to France has been so exactly fulfilled.
Aunt and uncle send their love, and desire
me to express their regret at the blow you
will receive in this letter. They intend
remaining here until your answer arrives.
With much love and sympathy,

Your ever affectionate sister,

Fanny d'Arminges.

The "blow" thus communicated had
precisely the opposite effect to that which
O'Rorke's sister and friends apprehended.
Instead of prostrating the recipient with
grief at the lady's perfidy, and kindling a
furnace of fury against the successful
rival, it roused a feeling of satisfaction
and delight quite uncommon in a jilted
lover. Instead of preying upon his mind,
it removed a load therefrom; and instead
of breaking his heart, it severed at once a

bond that for some considerable period he had contemplated with trouble and perplexity. In fact, this timely and welcome "blow" seemed to be the one essential remedy, as subsequent events testified, in effecting the invalid's convalescence. The engagement between O'Rorke and Eileen was evidently one in which fancy tied the slack and clumsy knot, whilst love stood idly looking on.

O'Rorke had not informed Gytha of his engagement; and Gytha was unaware that anything more serious than a "cousinly attachment" had ever existed between the two, until Madame d'Arminges mentioned to her that the tie was broken, and Eileen was married to Captain Wilmott.

Before, however, O'Rorke's returning strength would admit of his return to London, he heard from his sister that Gytha had left England for her home in Algiers. While chafing at the increasing distance that lay between them, he vowed to himself that not many weeks should elapse before he would again stand at her side. But when sufficiently recovered to carry out his purpose, he was obliged to defer so doing, on account of his sister, who wished him to go with her to France, there to wait the termination of the siege.

CHAPTER XIV.

"A lady-witch there lived on Atlas' mountain,
Within a cavern by a secret fountain."
The Witch of Atlas.

SUPINELY stretched under a wayside sycamore's " honied shade," lay a scantily clothed Arab boy, lazily tapping a caffre drum beside him, whilst his dusky eyes as lazily watched the lateen-sails skimming over the sunny bright waters of the Mediterranean. His quick ear catching the sound of distant footsteps, he turned his gaze down the road, in the direction whence they came. In the far distance he descried the approaching pedestrian.

For half a minute he looked intently, then sprang to his feet, and, with no unskilful hand, began beating the drum, breaking into an Arabic love-song as he neared the European.

"Catch, then, my dusky drummer," said the latter, as, in response to the boy's importunity, he tossed a silver coin into the air.

The next minute it was tightly clutched in a swarthy palm, and the musician, having gabbled his thanks, commenced a third stanza, his bare ebon feet keeping pace the while with the well-shod ones of his patron. "No, no, my boy. I've no wish to march to your drum," he said, with gesticulatory repulse.

Hearing horses' hoofs close behind, the boy was fain to obey the command, and turned in the hope of another chance coin being thrown to him by the rider; which hope was dispelled by a glance up into his face, by no means a strange one to the young Arab.

"Get out o' the way, ye lazy young

rascallion!" bade the horseman, cracking his whip.

At the sound of his shrill voice, the pedestrian halted and looked round.

"Hech! Master O'Rorke it is. Wha would hae thought o' seeing yoursel over here in this countree!" greeted Thrupp, reining in his horse as he reached the other's side.

"In whose topography I am not well versed. I was just wondering whether I was rightly following the direction given me. Am I on the road to the Villa Philœ?"

"Ye are on the right road, sir, but ye are going frae the house. Ye should hae turned up that road," he said, wheeling his horse sharply round, and pointing to a distant turning.

"Aha, I see—well, I've not gone far out of my way. I suppose you have just come from there—is Miss Keppel at home?"

"Aye, sir, I left her in the grot na' ten

minutes ago. There's an entrance off this road that wad take ye there sooner than t'other. I will gae back so far wi' ye."

"I can scarcely believe that it is the month of February!" exclaimed O'Rorke, lifting his hat to let the sea-breeze cool his temples, as he strode along by the side of the horse, a grey Arabian, on whose symmetry and step he admiringly remarked.

On reaching the postern-gate, Thrupp said he would go with him to a certain point from which he could direct him to the cave, and, dismounting, he led the horse within, and secured the reins to one of the posts.

Leaving him with his wet nose buried in the long grass, they plunged into the cool green shade of the abounding maple-trees; soon turning from the footpath, they threaded their way through a thicket of flowering myrtle, cactus, and rose-laurel.

Emerging from this fragrant wilderness, they mounted a gentle grassy slope; and now O'Rorke could see the gleaming walls of the Villa Philœ, surrounded by terraced grounds, beautiful with leafy shade, liquid sparkle, flowery maze, and grassy sweep.

O'Rorke had never before felt so thankfully mindful of the fortune his father's professional and speculative successes had accumulated, as now, while viewing the fair possessions of her he hoped to call his wife.

"Yon's the *Serena's* ascending-ground, and there her bit housie," broke in Thrupp's voice.

With much interest O'Rorke looked away at the "bit housie" sheltering the waif of the North Sea, and the marble flagged space from whence she had so often soared to aerial heights. As he pictured the ascent—the aspiring white and crimson sphere, the exultant-eyed aeronaut in her car—he looked above and around him. There on his right rose the green-clad, white-capped Atlas; there on his left spread the sail-dotted sea, on which she had gazed from her elevation.

Once more Thrupp's whip was raised.

" Ye see that gro'e—ye maun ga throu' that, then keep alang by that belt o' palms until you come to the burn, an's ye follow it up the brae, ye will see the mouth o' the grot. Do ye think ye will know now, sir ? "

Thanked and assured that his indications were not to be mistaken, he touched his cap and set off at a smart run down the slope ; while O'Rorke proceeded to follow his directions, soon reaching the olive grove.

> " I cannot see what flowers are at my feet,
>   Nor what soft incense hangs upon the boughs,"

he might have said, as he passed beneath their shade-casting density. But instead he muttered with a half-smile,—

R

" Surely some of the witches' ' loosed and missioned ' odours, must have winged their way hither ! "

On passing out into the brilliant sunshine, a splendid great butterfly, lightsome as the air, blue as the sky, crossed his path, pursuing its flight towards a thicket of tall Mediterranean heath, among whose plumy white blossoms he watched its azure beauty disappear.

Quickening his pace, he followed the guidance of the belt of palms. On his right hand the ground rose in a rocky acclivity, towards a darkly-wooded mountain-spur. And now a silver line, the clue to the witch's cave, flashed on his sight. In a few minutes he stood beside the stream

> " Of white and dancing waters all besprent
> With sand and polished pebbles."

Its joyous, hurried rush seemed to beat time to his heart's quick pulsations as he approached the rocky heights, where his eye had detected a portal shaded with acacias.

" Within a cavern by a secret fountain,"

he repeated. Then with a derisive laugh, " By the powers, I shall be thinking presently it is the original witch that I am in search of, and shall be expecting to find her

'Spelling out scrolls of dread antiquity.'

But what will she be doing, I wonder? Will she be annoyed at my unceremonious ·intrusion ? "

His dubious expression gave place to blank disappointment as on reaching the entrance and looking into

" The deep recesses of her odorous dwelling,"

he saw no wizard dweller! The only eyes that met his were those of a snowy owl in a niche of the rocky wall.

" A snowy creation of the witch," he mused, as he tarried on the threshold.

Near at hand stood a hammock-chair, a

rustic combination of unbarked wood and woven grass, over which was thrown a Cyprus scarf which he had last seen folded around her shoulders as she strolled about the prim garden at Chilworth. The glow of a fire in a distant alcove next attracted his gaze. Doubtless from thence came the subtle fragrance that pervaded the air. From the fire, his eyes came back to the littered table—a slice from the bole of a cedar-tree—and leisurely noted the various articles thereon; a solar microscope; a Phœnician lamp; an open book; a—his glance changed into a startled gaze —half-emptied box of *chico cigarros !*

No longer pleasurably curious, but apprehensively investigative, his eyes continued their examination—the shell of a Nautilus Pompilius, its pearly concavity partially filled with a crimson liquid; a large leaf on which lay a little heap of ashes and some cigarrette ends; a Nile flute, and a box of vestas.

That was all; but more than enough to destroy O'Rorke's peace of mind.

Whose recent presence did these things denote? Who had heaped those ashes, and quaffed from that oceanic goblet? Who had occupied the second of the two chairs?

With an abruptness that caused the owl to flutter and hoot, he strode within and caught up the volume, whose open pages showed Spanish poetry. Waiting not to acquaint himself with its title, he turned to the fly-leaf:—

"*From Gytha to her beloved Gio'.*"

Long and bitterly he looked at the inscription—death-warrant of his hopes—conceiving to his own misery and self-derision the happiness, the triumph, these words held for another—for "her beloved Gio'."

"Tuwhoo!" cried the owl, "Tu-whoo—o—o!"

Hurling an imprecation at the bird, he

laid down the book and turned to leave the cave; his love's instinct urging him to hasten from the torture of clasping the hand that had penned those words—of meeting the eyes that had reflected their tender import. But suddenly he halted, remembering Thrupp, and the improbability of her remaining in ignorance of his visit hither. "Well, since I must see her, it shall be at the Villa—anywhere rather than *here*."

He had taken but a pace, when again he halted.

She stood in the entrance.

As she stood, with the light behind her, he could not clearly see her face, which was moreover shaded by a palmetto hat. Gathered in one arm she held a mass of scarlet-flowered pimpernel, which here and there escaped its confine, and trailed down the pale amber-coloured dress, that fell in soft folds about her motionless figure.

"*You !*"—how her naïve exclamation

thrilled him. "This is a pleasant surprise. I wondered who Fatima could be hooting at so angrily," and once again her hand met his.

"I hope you will not, like her, resent this intrusion. I met Thrupp on the road, and he said you were in the grot; whither he was good enough to direct me."

"Then you have not been to the house—but do sit down, Mr. O'Rorke," she broke off, as she noticed his pallor. And motioning him to the chair by the table, she seated herself in the one whereon hung the scarf; "I have been so anxious for a letter from your sister; but doubtless you come from Paris, as she told me in her last letter you were going to accompany her to the environs, in readiness to enter as soon as the siege was over."

"Yes, we were there full three weeks waiting. I feared Fan whould fret herself into a fever."

"The delay must have been most trying

to her! And how did you find M. d'Arminges?"

"Still in the flesh—what there was left of it! He struck me as looking years older and inches taller than when I last saw him," he answered, wishing he could keep his thoughts from the obnoxious cigarettes at his elbow.

"He did not of course know you were coming?"

"No, we went straight to the *Ambulance Internationale,* where we found him helping to administer nourishment to the poor fellows. As soon as Fan had recovered from her burst of tears at the first sight of him, she was for plying him with some of the creature comforts from the ample basket we had brought with us. But he assured her he had already appeased his cravings, and begged her to hasten to Madame Raboteau. I guessed he was anxious to get her out of the infected air, but she straightway concluded that her friend was on the point of starvation, so away we went to the Hôtel Wagram, Fanny hugging a parcel of candles, for, as you doubtless know, the Parisians had sat in darkness—and I carrying the ample basket, feeling uncommonly like a Cockney mechanic bound for a day's outing with his missis. We were glad to find, on arriving there, that Mr. Washbourne had been beforehand with us in supplying her immediate wants. Aimée gleefully apprised me of the fact that they had just had some *real* beef, and *white* bread for dinner. Whereupon I told her to search in my pockets for her dessert; and on finding it in the form of *bonbons*, she declared she had not had a *bonbon* for years—not since Mamzelle Keppel gave her a box."

"Poor little dear! And where was Derry? did he go with you?" she asked, thinking of the anxious time when Aimée had first talked to her of him.

"No, his mother feared he might incur

infection at the *Ambulance.*　I told Aimée, thinking to please her, that she would see him the next day, but to my astonishment she burst out crying.　At length I drew from her, that Délie—the cat he had asked her to take care of—had strayed away one morning, and never returned !　And Susanne had told her that Délie had been killed and eaten, like the performing elephant, and the swans they used to feed with biscuits, and the donkeys they used to ride."

"Isn't it horrible to think of !　And madame, how was she ? "

"Well, she was up and about, but a woman of less ' grit ' would have taken to her bed.　And I think she would not have been able to hold out much longer.　She said she had been so hopeful back in November, when D'Arminges told her General Trochu had received a pigeon-telegram from Gambetta, proposing that the Loire and Paris armies should join forces. But when, after all its opening promises, the great sortie came to nought, she lost heart altogether, not so much on her own account as her mother's, whose life, she knew, depended on the nourishment that was becoming unprocurable."

"Poor Madame—what an agony of anxiety she must have suffered! How is the old lady?"

"I am sorry to say she died about a week before the capitulation!"

"Oh—not from privation?"

"Yes, that's what it was; the food they managed to exist on was not of a quality to sustain her."

Gytha was silent. The thought of her warm-hearted *garde-malade* helplessly watching the poor old sufferer sink lower and lower as the weary days dragged by, pained her beyond words.

He saw the tears slowly roll from beneath her drooping eyelids; and seeing, longed to kiss them away. But that privilege was another's, he himself must suffer them to roll down her cheeks, and drop like scalding lead on his heart.

Suddenly she looked up, her eyes to his surprise flashing indignation through their liquid grief.

"That General d'Aurelles deserves as severe a fate as any deserter!" she exclaimed bitterly.

"It's most maddening to think of the splendid opportunity he so obstinately threw away."

"Is your sister remaining in Paris?"

"Yes, at their old quarters, the Hôtel Wagram."

"Then Madame Raboteau will not want for a friend."

He was about to make a reply, when a shadow fell across, and a whiff of smoke floated by the entrance. The next moment the smoker appeared. But lo, a smoker wearing looped black skirts, and an elegantly disposed mantilla! Removing the cigarette from her lips, she was beginning in a voice of indolent annoyance,—

"Would you believe it, *cara mia*, that lovely azalea—" when her eyes fell on O'Rorke, in the act of rising.

"This is Mr. O'Rorke, Gio'," said Gytha; then, glancing at him, "My friend, Mrs. Meredith."

"Mr. O'Rorke! This is a pleasure I have greatly wished for," she said graciously.

"I feel honoured, madame," he said, inwardly execrating his own credulity, and the lady's masculine fancy, "this is your seat, I think," he added, stepping aside for her to pass to it.

"Thanks. Then will you take that camp-stool?" she said, with a graceful wave of her hand towards the stool, folded against the wall. Then sinking into the grass hammock, she listened sympathetically whilst Gytha told her of Madame Raboteau's bereavement.

" And how is the capital looking, Mr. O'Rorke ? "

Thus recalled from his reflections on the discovery that had revolutionized his feelings to their former hopefulness, he raised his eyes from the halfa matting to her dark and still handsome face.

" In the outskirts, as desolate as gutted houses, débris-heaped streets, and knots of homeless excavators, seeking their goods and chattles, can render it. But in the interior, lively with bevies of sight-seeking grisettes, and swarms of uniformed and bloused ' patriots.' I should not be surprised if there be a renewal of the October and January riots."

" Dear me ! they are belligerent, then, rather than subdued. I have been picturing them going about as sad-faced and clothed as the Sevillans in Lent."

" Oh, there is no scarcity of sad faces— and the gay and sad alike of the Parisiennes have put on mourning. That is the most striking reminder of the National calamity, even the very statues are crape-masked. To my eyes, they look like so many disguised burglars," he said, watching, as he spoke, the Witch's white fingers despoiling the trailing pimpernel stems of their leaves, which she dropped into a basket beside her.

A coloured youth now made his appearance, and in broken English informed Gytha that Pompey awaited her without.

"Pompey—oh, I had forgotten!" she paused ; then looking from the boy to O'Rorke, she told him she had promised to visit the ailing wife of a vine-dresser, who lived up on the mountain.

"I should be glad to accompany you as far," he said impulsively.

"But it is a long way, you will be tired. I would offer you another donkey, but we have only side-saddles."

On his assuring her he should much prefer walking, and declaring himself equal to any amount of that exercise, it was settled that he should accompany her.

Rising from her chair, Gytha brushed away the scarlet petals clinging to her dress.

" The jar is in there, Usimone; the one nearest this end," she said to the boy, whose supple figure O'Rorke's eyes followed to the indicated recess, where on a block of stone, several jars were ranged.

"That is Gytha's medicine-chest," smilingly said the elder lady, " she is very wise in herbal virtues and decoctions—that is a syrup of her preparation,"—inclining her head towards the shell. " And then there is the Enigma Brand, as I call it, for whoever drinks of it must first solve my riddle. My first, is a herb that breathes of a maiden; my second, a blossom, sacred to Hymen; my third, the tears of a crushed reed; and my whole, a syrup you must name."

" But perhaps I have never heard the name ! "

" I fancy you must have, it is a French beverage."

" I am afraid I shall never taste it," said he, with a laugh, after a few minutes' consideration.   But the words had scarcely left his lips, when he exclaimed, " Capillaire ! "

She laughed assent; and Gytha fetched an amethyst drinking-cup, and a glass jar from the recess.   Having filled the former, she handed it to him with the smiling remark, " I am sure you will not think the syrup so good as the riddle."

" Indeed it completely fulfils the enigma's sweet suggestions," he averred, on tasting the luscious drink.

" We dine at seven, Mr. O'Rorke. I hope you will give us the pleasure of your company," said Mrs. Meredith, when he took up his hat.

With an inward wonder as to whether

it would prolong a felicitous, or an embarrassing companionship, he accepted her invitation, and followed Gytha to a spot where Usimone was standing beside a shapely Egyptian donkey, whose bright eyes and forward bent ears, eloquently expressed his pleasure at the approach of his mistress.

" I would have put off going until to-morrow," said Gytha as O'Rorke reached her side, " but I promised the poor woman —or rather girl, for she is only sixteen— that I would take her some more pimpernel decoction this afternoon ; for, between pain and anxiety, she cannot sleep without the aid of a narcotic. She fears her husband has destroyed himself, under the impression that he had killed her. In a fit of jealousy he struck her with his pruning knife, and then rushed from the hut ; that was four days ago, and he has not been heard of since.

CHAPTER XV.

"Her soft smiles shone afar,
And her low voice was heard like love."
The Witch of Atlas.

"YEK, yek!" cried Usimone, as soon as she had mounted, and Pompey set off at a gentle pace, O'Rorke keeping at his side.

Before long the beaten track sharply rounded the spur, and after the intervention of a gate, continued up a pass, the sheer-rising, shrub-tufted walls of which cast

"Darkness and odours and a pleasure hid
In melancholy gloom."

"Rather a contraction of the celestial view we once commanded," said O'Rorke, glancing up at the rift of blue, scarcely

more than enough to define the shrubs
projecting near the summit of the rocks.
" What a glorious flight that was ! Times
out of number I have fallen asleep to
literally ' dream visions of aerial joy.'
Alas ! the bathos, to wake and find the
billowy cloud-layer reduced to a billowy
counterpane ! Have you made any captive
ascents since your return here ? "

" Not until a fortnight since, when I
made a little series, for the *Serena* remained inflated four days."

" I have been glad to think that captive
assents were all you would venture on here,
else I should have been continually fearing
you were in some perilous extremity,"
for the first time he voluntarily let his
tone express somewhat of his feelings.

The dark eyes looking up the pass filled
with a lovely light, that seemed to have
its dawn on the clear cheek he glanced at.

" Yek, yek, yek ! " again shrilly sounded
from behind, and again poor Pompey started

into a trot, whose briskness Gytha was obliged to moderate out of consideration for her companion.

Looking round, she saw him speaking to Usimone. "I have been telling that young whipper-in, that if Pompey is inclined to be stubborn again, I will give him ' sweet mouth,' " he said, smiling, as he came to her side.

" Which I can assure you he knows how to appreciate," she responded, stroking the glossy neck of the animal, whose clattering hoofs awoke echo upon echo— echoes that became fainter and fainter as the sterile walls gradually receded, until the pass widened into a wooded glen, open to the golden light of the westering sun. From the glen they mounted to a grassy tableland, overlooking a wheat-feathered basin, that lay shut in by mountains, varied with green growth, grey crags, purple recesses, and snow-gleaming pinnacles.

" How attached you must be to these

valleys and mountains!" he exclaimed, after a few moments' silent survey.

"I am indeed! They hold lifelong associations for me."

"Lifelong?" he repeated, in a tone of surprise.

"Yes, I'm an Algerine by birth. I was born the very first winter my father spent here. It was my poor mother's first and last. My only idea of her is drawn from this miniature," she added, unclasping from her neck a slight gold chain, and opening the attached locket, she gave it with the necklet, into his hand.

It was a face of blonde loveliness, high-bred imperiousness, on which his eyes fell. The only similarity in the portrayed features and those whose every curve and line were so impressed on his mind, was the mouth; there was the same sweeping arch of the upper lip, the same slight indentation of the nether. Enshrined in the back of the locket was finely braided hair of the same fairness as the pictured tresses.

"This is indeed, 'silent, penetrative loveliness,' " he quoted aloud, as he gazed. "But I did not expect to see a blonde," he added, looking up at her.

"Because I am dark—while she fully confirmed her Saxon descent."

"Ah! then that accounts for your Saxon name—Gytha." Then wondering at his boldness in pronouncing it, he went on quickly, "How much we owe to the limner's art! You must value this greatly!" returning it to her.

Pompey was now slowly following the bridle-path scraped out of the mountain side. The roar of falling water had for some time past prepared O'Rorke for the vision of beauty that the track's curvature now disclosed, to wit, one of those

> "Earthquaking cataracts which shiver
> Their snow-like waters into golden air."

Halting at O'Rorke's request, she

watched with him the shimmering waters dashing from a ledge of rocks, high on the opposite mountain, down into the bosky ravine. The last time she had solitarily tarried there, how keenly had her love-conscious spirit—" felt itself alone." Then her thoughts had brooded on a remark made by Madame d'Arminges in speaking of her brother's broken engagement. " I believe, though, judging from his letter, he doesn't feel it so keenly as I feared. I suppose it was a case of mere love-in-idleness with them both." And now that expression recurred to her mind, bringing with it a discordant doubt. Was the love that had swayed his voice and impassioned his glance, mere love-in-idleness ?

As he watched the glancing waters, a doubt—begotten of the knowledge that his sister had made such a remark—was also harassing his mind. Would he be able to convince her, that until her voice and smile had quickened his heart into

Love's glorious life, Fancy had been its deepest emotion?

"Water, big jump, big roar—say?" impatiently said Usimone, pausing in his exuberant skipping and looking at O'Rorke with round eyes of surprise at his silence.

"I fear Usimone thinks me sadly wanting in demonstration," said O'Rorke, turning with a dry smile to his mounted companion. "But, in faith, admiration closes my lips! How often the beauty of this will flash upon my 'inward eye' in time to come!"

"*In time to come!*" The words fell with an ominous chill on her heart, as an answer to its doubts of a minute since. And, making no answer, she shook her bridle.

A little further on, the path, rounding the shoulder of the mountain, brought them in sight of another cultivated valley.

The first feature that attracted O'Rorke's

eyes was the opposite ridge—the ridge over which he had watched the fair crescent rise. But where was the sombre mantle of the " Witch Mountain "—as he had called it ? it was but very shreds and patches of vegetation that she now wore.

" Surely a Cypress forest used to cover that mountain ? " he said, turning to Gytha.

" Yes, it did, but it was destroyed by fire three years ago. Gio' and I came here and watched it burning. It was a grand sight. The whole mountain was one sheet of flame ? every stone and shrub in the valley were as visible as by daylight. I wish—"

" Señorita ! " The voice came from above, and, looking up the slope, they saw a swarthy peasant, crouching among the shrubs, looking down on them with eager, black eyes.

" Ramiro ! " exclaimed Gytha, halting.

" For the blessed Virgin's sake, tell me

—Martina, is she alive?" he said in his native Spanish language.

"Yes, and fast recovering; I am on my way to her now."

"May your lips sing in paradise!" he ejaculated, and bowed his working face in his hand.

"And now, Ramiro, you will come with me to Martina," she said in a voice that blended "gentleness and power" into supple persuasion. Lifting his bowed head, the man looked down on her with eyes of intense wistfulness. The next moment he shook his head dejectedly.

"She would repel me with curses."

"Nay, she will receive you with gladness," she said with decision.

"I will go with you—I will show her my heart." So saying, he slid down the slope, and preceded Pompey up the steep, narrow track, now winding towards where vineyards displayed their bright green foliage. Before they reached these, however, the man halted, and Gytha checked the donkey, telling O'Rorke that she must now proceed on foot.

Ramiro having at her request taken the jar and basket from Usimone—whom they left to look after Pompey—they mounted the olive-grown slope. On gaining a plateau where stood a thatched hut, she told Ramiro she would go in first, and tell Martina that he was waiting without.

Seeing the man was absorbed in suspense, O'Rorke strolled to the edge of the plateau, and looked down on the valley of corn. The moon, that, when they started, had looked like a fragment of white cloud in the sunny sky, now seemed silverised into a luminous power, as the daylight rapidly faded.

He was lost in recalling every tone and expression that had varied her voice and face during her ride hither, when her low voice fell on his ear.

"We can return now." And turning, he saw her approaching, her dark eyes softly radiant.

"So the breach is healed—they are united again," he said, as they began to descend the root-matted, olive-shaded slope.

"Yes, I am so glad, for poor little Martina's sake. I found her in utter despair—her rosary had broken, while she was repeating *aves* on his behalf, and she regarded it as an ill omen."

"Then I suspect she was not sorry to have her superstition shaken—what light is that?" he broke off, as he was passing an aged tree, in whose hollow trunk shone a pale green luminosity. "Ah! I see—the jewels some fair hamadryad has left here," he added, as on looking more closely he saw the light arose from a constellation of luminous beetles. And stooping over the decayed cavity, he gently raised one of the brilliant "jewels" from its mossy casket, and, bending on one knee, placed it in the buckle of her dainty shoe.

"That is too precarious a setting," she said with a smile, and, stooping, took the firefly in her hand, and dropped it into a fold of her Cyprus scarf, from whose transparent darkness it scintillated starry rays.

"Did the nymph but know jewel of hers adorns her much-loved Witch!" he exclaimed, highly pleased that she had exalted his lowly adornment to her heart. Would she but so receive his petition!

Meeting the wondering look she bent on him, he went on impetuously,—

"The Witch of Atlas—the Witch of love and power! Let that power verify the sweet visions that have gladdened my heart—visions wherein we have stood as now we stand, only that this hand of mine held yours, the hand of my love—my promised wife."

The next moment his waiting palm held her soft, pulsating hand, and with tender elation his lips sealed, and thrice sealed, the fair pledge.

THE END.

LONDON:
PRINTED BY GILBERT AND RIVINGTON, LIMITED,
ST. JOHN'S HOUSE, CLERKENWELL ROAD.

𝔄 𝔖election from the 𝔏ist of 𝔅ooks

PUBLISHED BY

SAMPSON LOW, MARSTON, SEARLE, & RIVINGTON,

LIMITED.

Low's Standard Novels, page 17.
Low's Standard Books for Boys, page 18.
Low's Standard Series, page 19.
Sea Stories, by W. CLARK RUSSELL, page 26.

ALPHABETICAL LIST.

ABBEY and Parsons, Quiet life. From drawings; the motive by Austin Dobson, 4to.

Abney (W. de W.) and Cunningham. Pioneers of the Alps. With photogravure portraits of guides. Imp. 8vo, gilt top, 21*s.*

Adam (G. Mercer) and Wetherald. An Algonquin Maiden. Crown 8vo, 5*s.*

Alcott. Works of the late Miss Louisa May Alcott :—
Aunt Jo's Scrap-bag. Cloth, 2*s.*
Eight Cousins. Illustrated, 2*s.*; cloth gilt, 3*s.* 6*d.*
Jack and Jill. Illustrated, 2*s.*; cloth gilt, 3*s.* 6*d.*
Jo's Boys. 5*s.*
Jimmy's Cruise in the Pinafore, &c. Illustrated, cloth, 2*s.*; gilt edges, 3*s.* 6*d.*
Little Men. Double vol., 2*s.*; cloth, gilt edges, 3*s.* 6*d.*
Little Women. 1*s.* ⎱ 1 vol., cloth, 2*s.* ; larger ed., gilt
Little Women Wedded. 1*s.* ⎰ edges, 3*s.* 6*d.*
Old-fashioned Girl. 2*s.*; cloth, gilt edges, 3*s.* 6*d.*
Rose in Bloom. 2*s.*; cloth gilt, 3*s.* 6*d.*
Shawl Straps. Cloth, 2*s.*
Silver Pitchers. Cloth, gilt edges, 3*s.* 6*d.*
Under the Lilacs. Illustrated, 2*s* ; cloth gilt, 5*s.*
Work : a Story of Experience 1*s.* ⎱ 1 vol., cloth, gilt
—— Its Sequel, "Beginning Again." 1*s.* ⎰ edges, 3*s.* 6*d.*
—— *Life, Letters and Journals.* By EDNAH D. CHENEY. Cr. 8vo, 6*s.*
—— See also "Low's Standard Series."

Alden (W. L.) Adventures of Jimmy Brown, written by himself. Illustrated. Small crown 8vo, cloth, 2*s.*
—— *Trying to find Europe.* Illus., crown 8vo, 5*s.*

A

Alger (J. G.) Englishmen in the French Revolution, cr. 8vo, 7s. 6d.

Amateur Angler's Days in Dove Dale : Three Weeks' Holiday in 1884. By E. M. 1s. 6d.; boards, 1s.; large paper, 5s.

Andersen. Fairy Tales. An entirely new Translation. With over 500 Illustrations by Scandinavian Artists. Small 4to, 6s.

Anderson (W.) Pictorial Arts of Japan. With 80 full-page and other Plates, 16 of them in Colours. Large imp. 4to, £8 8s. (in four folio parts, £2 2s. each); Artists' Proofs, £12 12s.

Angling. See Amateur, "Cutcliffe," "Fennell," "Halford," "Hamilton," "Martin," "Orvis," "Pennell," "Pritt," "Senior," "Stevens," "Theakston," "Walton," "Wells," and "Willis-Bund."

Arnold (R.) Ammonia and Ammonium Compounds. Translated, illus., crown 8vo, 5s.

Art Education. See "Biographies," "D'Anvers," "Illustrated Text Books," "Mollett's Dictionary."

Artistic Japan. Illustrated with Coloured Plates. Monthly. Royal 4to, 2s.; vol. I., 15s.; II., roy. 4to., 15s.

Ashe (R. P.) Two Kings of Uganda ; Six Years in E. Equa- torial Africa. Crown 8vo, 6s.

Attwell (Prof.) The Italian Masters. Crown 8vo, 3s. 6d.

Audsley (G. A.) Handbook of the Organ. Imperial 8vo, top edge gilt, 31s. 6d.; large paper, 63s.

—— *Ornamental Arts of Japan.* 90 Plates, 74 in Colours and Gold, with General and Descriptive Text. 2 vols., folio, £15 15s.; in specally designed leather, £23 2s.

—— *The Art of Chromo-Lithography.* Coloured Plates and Text. Folio, 63s.

BACON (Delia) Biography, with Letters of Carlyle, Emerson, &c. Crown 8vo, 10s. 6d.

Baddeley (W. St. Clair) Tchay and Chianti. Small 8vo, 5s.

—— *Travel-tide.* Small post 8vo, 7s. 6d.

Baldwin (James) Story of Siegfried. 6s.

—— *Story of the Golden Age.* Illustrated by HOWARD PYLE. Crown 8vo, 6s.

—— *Story of Roland.* Crown 8vo, 6s.

Bamford (A. J.) Turbans and Tails. Sketches in the Un- romantic East. Crown 8vo, 7s. 6d.

Barlow (Alfred) Weaving by Hand and by Power. With several hundred Illustrations. Third Edition, royal 8vo, £1 5s.

Barlow (P. W.) Kaipara, Experiences of a Settler in N. New Zealand. Illust., crown 8vo, 6s.

Bassett (F. S.) Legends and Superstitions of the Sea. 7s. 6d.

THE BAYARD SERIES.

Edited by the late J. HAIN FRISWELL.

Comprising Pleasure Books of Literature produced in the Choicest Style.

"We can hardly imagine better books for boys to read or for men to ponder over."—*Times.*

Price 2s. 6d. each Volume, complete in itself, flexible cloth extra, gilt edges, with silk Headbands and Registers.

The Story of the Chevalier Bayard.
Joinville's St. Louis of France.
The Essays of Abraham Cowley.
Abdallah. By Edouard Laboullaye.
Napoleon, Table-Talk and Opinions.
Words of Wellington.
Johnson's Rasselas. With Notes.
Hazlitt's Round Table.
The Religio Medici, Hydriotaphia, &c. By Sir Thomas Browne, Knt.
Coleridge's Christabel, &c. With Preface by Algernon C. Swinburne.
Ballad Poetry of the Affections. By Robert Buchanan.
Lord Chesterfield's Letters, Sentences, and Maxims. With Essay by Sainte-Beuve.
The King and the Commons. Cavalier and Puritan Songs.
Vathek. By William Beckford.
Essays in Mosaic. By Ballantyne.
My Uncle Toby; his Story and his Friends. By P. Fitzgerald.
Reflections of Rochefoucauld.
Socrates: Memoirs for English Readers from Xenophon's Memorabilia. By Edw. Levien.
Prince Albert's Golden Precepts.

A Case containing 12 Volumes, price 31s. 6d.; or the Case separately, price 3s. 6d.

Beaugrand (C.) Walks Abroad of Two Young Naturalists. By D. SHARP. Illust., 8vo, 7s. 6d.

Beecher (H. W.) Authentic Biography, and Diary. Ill. 8vo, 21s.

Behnke and Browne. Child's Voice: its Treatment with regard to After Development. Small 8vo, 3s. 6d.

Bell (H. H. J.) Obeah: Negro Superstition in the West Indies. Crown 8vo, 2s. 6d.

Beyschlag. Female Costume Figures of various Centuries. 12 reproductions of pastel designs in portfolio, imperial. 21s.

Bickerdyke (J.) Irish Midsummer Night's Dream. Illus. by E. M. COX. Crown 8vo, 1s. 6d.; boards, 1s.

Bickersteth (Bishop E. H.) Clergyman in his Home. 1s.

————— *Evangelical Churchmanship.* 1s.

————— *From Year to Year: Original Poetical Pieces.* Small post 8vo, 3s. 6d.; roan, 6s. and 5s.; calf or morocco, 10s. 6d.

————— *The Master's Home-Call.* N. ed. 32mo, cloth gilt, 1s.

————— *The Master's Will.* A Funeral Sermon preached on the Death of Mrs. S. Gurney Buxton. Sewn, 6d.; cloth gilt, 1s.

————— *The Reef, and other Parables.* Crown 8vo, 2s. 6d.

————— *Shadow of the Rock.* Select Religious Poetry. 2s. 6d.

————— *Shadowed Home and the Light Beyond.* 5s.

————— See also "Hymnal Companion."

Biographies of the Great Artists (Illustrated). Crown 8vo, emblematical binding, 3s. 6d. per volume, except where the price is given.

Claude le Lorrain, by Owen J. Dullea.

Correggio, by M. E. Heaton. 2s. 6d.

Della Robbia and Cellini. 2s. 6d.

Albrecht Dürer, by R. F. Heath.

Figure Painters of Holland.

Fra Angelico, Masaccio, and Botticelli.

Fra Bartolommeo, Albertinelli, and Andrea del Sarto.

Gainsborough and Constable.

Ghiberti and Donatello. 2s. 6d.

Giotto, by Harry Quilter.

Hans Holbein, by Joseph Cundall.

Hogarth, by Austin Dobson.

Landseer, by F. G. Stevens.

Lawrence and Romney, by Lord Ronald Gower. 2s. 6d.

Leonardo da Vinci.

Little Masters of Germany, by W. B. Scott.

Mantegna and Francia.

Meissonier, by J. W. Mollett. 2s. 6d.

Michelangelo Buonarotti, by Clément.

Murillo, by Ellen E. Minor. 2s. 6d.

Overbeck, by J. B. Atkinson.

Raphael, by N. D'Anvers.

Rembrandt, by J. W. Mollett.

Reynolds, by F. S. Pulling.

Rubens, by C. W. Kett.

Tintoretto, by W. R. Osler.

Titian, by R. F. Heath.

Turner, by Cosmo Monkhouse.

Vandyck and Hals, by P. R. Head.

Velasquez, by E. Stowe.

Vernet and Delaroche, by J. Rees.

Watteau, by J. W. Mollett. 2s. 6d.

Wilkie, by J. W. Mollett.

IN PREPARATION.

Barbizon School, by J. W. Mollett.

Cox and De Wint, Lives and Works.

George Cruikshank, Life and Works.

Miniature Painters of Eng. School.

Mulready Memorials, by Stephens.

Van de Velde and the Dutch Painters.

Bird (F. J.) American Practical Dyer's Companion. 8vo, 42s.

———— *(H. E.) Chess Practice.* 8vo, 2s. 6d.

Black (Robert) Horse Racing in France : a History. 8vo, 14s.

———— See also CICERO.

Black (W.) Penance of John Logan, and other Tales. Crown 8vo, 10s. 6d.

————See also " Low's Standard Library."

Blackburn (Charles F.) Hints on Catalogue Titles and Index Entries, with a Vocabulary of Terms and Abbreviations, chiefly from Foreign Catalogues. Royal 8vo, 14s.

Blackburn (Henry) Art in the Mountains, the Oberammergau Passion Play. New ed., corrected to date, 8vo, 5s.

———— *Breton Folk.* With 171 Illust. by RANDOLPH CALDECOTT Imperial 8vo, gilt edges, 21s.; plainer binding, 10s. 6d.

———— *Pyrenees.* Illustrated by GUSTAVE DORÉ, corrected to 1881. Crown 8vo, 7s. 6d. See also CALDECOTT.

Blackmore (R. D.) Kit and Kitty. A novel. 3 vols., crown 8vo, 31s. 6d.

———— *Lorna Doone. Edition de luxe.* Crown 4to, very numerous Illustrations, cloth, gilt edges, 31s. 6d.; parchment, uncut, top gilt, 35s.; new issue, plainer, 21s.

———— *Novels.* See also " Low's Standard Novels."

Blackmore (R. D.) Springhaven. Illust. by PARSONS and BARNARD. Sq. 8vo, 12*s.*; new edition, 7*s.* 6*d.*

Blaikie (William) How to get Strong and how to Stay so. Rational, Physical, Gymnastic, &c., Exercises. Illust., sm. post 8vo, 5*s.*

———— *Sound Bodies for our Boys and Girls.* 16mo, 2*s.* 6*d.*

Bonwick. British Colonies. Asia, 1*s.*; Africa, 1*s.*; America, 1*s.*; Australasia, 1*s.* One vol., cloth, 5*s.*

Bosanquet (Rev. C.) Blossoms from the King's Garden : Sermons for Children. 2nd Edition, small post 8vo, cloth extra, 6*s.*

———— *Jehoshaphat ; or, Sunlight and Clouds.* 1*s.*

Bowden (H.; Miss) Witch of the Atlas : a ballooning story, Crown 8vo, 6*s.*

Bower (G. S.) and Spencer, Law of Electric Lighting. New edition, crown 8vo, 12*s.* 6*d.*

Boyesen (H. H.) Modern Vikings : Stories of Life and Sport in Norseland. Cr. 8vo, 6*s.*

———— *Story of Norway.* Illustrated, sm. 8vo, 7*s.* 6*d.*

Boy's Froissart. King Arthur. Knightly Legends of Wales. Percy. See LANIER.

Bradshaw (J.) New Zealand as it is. 8vo, 12*s.* 6*d.*

———— *New Zealand of To-day,* 1884-87. 8vo, 14*s.*

Brannt (W. T.) Animal and Vegetable Fats and Oils. Illust., 8vo, 35*s.*

———— *Manufacture of Soap and Candles, with many Formulas.* Illust., 8vo, 35*s.*

———— *Manufacture of Vinegar, Cider, and Fruit Wines.* Illustrated, 8vo.

———— *Metallic Alloys. Chiefly from the German of Krupp* and Wildberger. Crown 8vo, 12*s.* 6*d.*

Bright (John) Public Letters. Crown 8vo, 7*s.* 6*d.*

Brisse (Baron) Ménus (366). A *ménu,* in French and English, for every Day in the Year. 2nd Edition. Crown 8vo, 5*s.*

Brittany. See BLACKBURN.

Browne (G. Lennox) Voice Use and Stimulants. Sm. 8vo, 3*s.* 6*d.*

———— *and Behnke (Emil) Voice, Song, and Speech.* N. ed., 5*s.*

Brumm (C.) Bismarck, his Deeds and Aims; reply to "Bismarck Dynasty." 8vo, 1*s.*

Bruntie's Diary. A Tour round the World. By C. E. B., 1*s.* 6*d.*

Bryant (W. C.) and Gay (S. H.) History of the United States 4 vols., royal 8vo, profusely Illustrated, 60*s.*

Bryce (Rev. Professor) Manitoba. Illust. Crown 8vo, 7*s.* 6*d.*

———— *Short History of the Canadian People.* 7*s.* 6*d.*

Bulkeley (Owen T.) Lesser Antilles. Pref. by D. MORRIS. Illus., crown 8vo, boards, 2*s.* 6*d.*

Burnaby (Mrs. F.) High Alps in Winter; or, Mountaineering
in Search of Health. With Illustrations, &c., 14*s.* See also MAIN.
Burnley (J.) History of the Silk Trade.
—— *History of Wool and Woolcombing.* Illust. 8vo, 21*s.*
Burton (Sir R. F.) Early, Public, and Private Life. Edited
by F. HITCHMAN. 2 vols., 8vo, 36*s.*
Butler (Sir W. F.) Campaign of the Cataracts. Illust., 8vo, 18*s.*
—— *Invasion of England, told twenty years after.* 2*s.* 6*d.*
—— *Red Cloud ; or, the Solitary Sioux.* Imperial 16mo,
numerous illustrations, gilt edges, 3*s.* 6*d.*; plainer binding, 2*s.* 6*d.*
—— *The Great Lone Land ; Red River Expedition.* 7*s.* 6*d.*
—— *The Wild North Land; the Story of a Winter Journey*
with Dogs across Northern North America. 8vo, 18*s.* Cr. 8vo, 7*s.* 6*d.*
Bynner (E. L.) Agnes Surriage. Crown 8vo, 10*s.* 6*d.*

*C*ABLE *(G. W.) Bonaventure : A Prose Pastoral of Acadian*
Louisiana. Sm. post 8vo, 5*s.*
Cadogan (Lady A.) Drawing-room Plays. 10*s.* 6*d.* ; acting ed.,
6*d.* each.
—— *Illustrated Games of Patience.* Twenty-four Diagrams
in Colours, with Text. Fcap. 4to, 12*s.* 6*d.*
—— *New Games of Patience.* Coloured Diagrams, 4to, 12*s.* 6*d.*
Caldecott (Randolph) Memoir. By HENRY BLACKBURN. With
170 Examples of the Artist's Work. 14*s.*; new edit., 7*s.* 6*d.*
—— *Sketches.* With an Introduction by H. BLACKBURN.
4to, picture boards, 2*s.* 6*d.*
California. See NORDHOFF.
Callan (H.) Wanderings on Wheel and on Foot. Cr. 8vo, 1*s.* 6*d.*
Campbell (Lady Colin) Book of the Running Brook : and of
Still Waters. 5*s.*
Canadian People : Short History. Crown 8vo, 7*s.* 6*d.*
Carbutt (Mrs.) Five Months' Fine Weather in Canada,
West U.S., and Mexico. Crown 8vo, 5*s.*
Carleton, City Legends. Special Edition, illus., royal 8vo,
12*s.* 6*d.* ; ordinary edition, crown 8vo, 1*s.*
—— *City Ballads.* Illustrated, 12*s.* 6*d.* New Ed. (Rose
Library), 16mo, 1*s.*
—— *Farm Ballads, Farm Festivals, and Farm Legends.*
Paper boards, 1*s.* each ; 1 vol., small post 8vo, 3*s.* 6*d.*
Carnegie (A.) American Four-in-Hand in Britain. Small
4to, Illustrated, 10*s.* 6*d.* Popular Edition, paper, 1*s.*
—— *Round the World.* 8vo, 10*s.* 6*d.*
—— *Triumphant Democracy.* 6*s.* ; also 1*s.* 6*d.* and 1*s.*
Chairman's Handbook. By R. F. D. PALGRAVE. 5th Edit., 2*s.*

Changed Cross, &c. Religious Poems. 16mo, 2s. 6d.; calf, 6s.

Chess. See BIRD (H. E.).

Children's Praises. Hymns for Sunday-Schools and Services.
Compiled by LOUISA H. H. TRISTRAM. 4d.

Choice Editions of Choice Books. 2s. 6d. each. Illustrated by
C. W. COPE, R.A., T. CRESWICK, R.A., E. DUNCAN, BIRKET
FOSTER, J. C. HORSLEY, A.R.A., G. HICKS, R. REDGRAVE, R.A.,
C. STONEHOUSE, F. TAYLER, G. THOMAS, H. J. TOWNSHEND,
E. H. WEHNERT, HARRISON WEIR, &c.

Bloomfield's Farmer's Boy.	Milton's L'Allegro.
Campbell's Pleasures of Hope.	Poetry of Nature. Harrison Weir.
Coleridge's Ancient Mariner.	Rogers' (Sam.) Pleasures of Memory.
Goldsmith's Deserted Village.	Shakespeare's Songs and Sonnets.
Goldsmith's Vicar of Wakefield.	Tennyson's May Queen.
Gray's Elegy in a Churchyard.	Elizabethan Poets.
Keats' Eve of St. Agnes.	Wordsworth's Pastoral Poems.

"Such works are a glorious beatification for a poet."—*Athenæum.*

Christ in Song. By PHILIP SCHAFF. New Ed., gilt edges, 6s.

Chromo-Lithography. See AUDSLEY.

Cicero, Tusculan Disputation, I. (Death no bane). Translated
by R. BLACK. Small crown 8vo.

Clarke (H. P.) See WILLS.

Clarke (P.) Three Diggers: a Tale of the Australian Fifties.
Crown 8vo, 6s.

Cochran (W.) Pen and Pencil in Asia Minor. Illust., 8vo, 21s.

Collingwood (Harry) Under the Meteor Flag. The Log of a
Midshipman. Illustrated, small post 8vo, gilt, 3s. 6d.; plainer, 2s. 6d.

—— *Voyage of the "Aurora."* Gilt, 3s. 6d.; plainer, 2s. 6d.

Collinson (Sir R.; Adm.) H.M.S. "Enterprise" in search of Sir
J. Franklin. 8vo.

Colonial Year-book. Edited and compiled by A. J. R.
TRENDELL. Crown 8vo, 6s.

Cook (Dutton) Book of the Play. New Edition. 1 vol., 3s. 6d.

—— *On the Stage: Studies.* 2 vols., 8vo, cloth, 24s.

Cozzens (F.) American Yachts. 27 Plates, 22 × 28 inches.
Proofs, £21; Artist's Proofs, £31 10s.

Craddock (C. E.) Despot of Broomsedge Cove. Crown 8vo, 6s.

Crew (B. J.) Practical Treatise on Petroleum. Illust., 8vo, 28s.

Crouch (A. P.) Glimpses of Feverland: a Cruise in West African
Waters. Crown 8vo, 6s.

—— *On a Surf-bound Coast.* Crown 8vo, 7s. 6d.

Cumberland (Stuart) Thought Reader's Thoughts. Cr. 8vo., 10s. 6d.

—— *Queen's Highway from Ocean to Ocean.* Ill., 8vo, 18s.;
new ed., 7s. 6d.

Cumberland (S.) Vasty deep : a Strange Story of To-day. New Edition, 6s.

Cundall (Joseph). See "Remarkable Bindings."

Cushing (W.) Initials and Pseudonyms. Large 8vo, 25s.; second series, large 8vo, 21s.

Custer (Eliz. B.) Tenting on the Plains; Gen. Custer in Kansas and Texas. Royal 8vo, 18s.

Cutcliffe (H. C.) Trout Fishing in Rapid Streams. Cr. 8vo, 3s. 6d.

DALY (Mrs. D.) Digging, Squatting, and Pioneering in Northern South Australia. 8vo, 12s.

D'Anvers. Elementary History of Art. New ed., 360 illus., 2 vols., cr. 8vo. I. Architecture, &c., 5s.; II. Painting, 6s.; 1 vol., 10s. 6d.

—— *Elementary History of Music.* Crown 8vo, 2s. 6d.

Davis (Clement) Modern Whist. 4s.

—— *(C. T.) Bricks, Tiles, Terra-Cotta, &c.* N. ed. 8vo, 25s.

—— *Manufacture of Leather.* With many Illustrations. 52s. 6d.

—— *Manufacture of Paper.* 28s.

—— *(G. B.) Outlines of International Law.* 8vo. 10s. 6d.

Dawidowsky. Glue, Gelatine, Isinglass, Cements, &c. 8vo, 12s. 6d.

Day of My Life at Eton. By an ETON BOY. New ed. 16mo, 1s.

Day's Collacon : an Encyclopædia of Prose Quotations. Imperial 8vo, cloth, 31s. 6d.

De Leon (E.) Under the Stars and under the Crescent. N. ed., 6s.

Dethroning Shakspere. Letters to the Daily Telegraph ; and Editorial Papers. Crown 8vo, 2s. 6d.

Dickinson (Charles M.) The Children, and other Verses. Sm. 8vo, gilt edges, 5s.

Dictionary. See TOLHAUSEN, "Technological."

Diggle (J. W.; Canon) Lancashire Life of Bishop Fraser. 8vo, 12s. 6d.

Donnelly (Ignatius) Atlantis ; or, the Antediluvian World. 7th Edition, crown 8vo, 12s. 6d.

—— *Ragnarok : The Age of Fire and Gravel.* Illustrated, crown 8vo, 12s. 6d.

—— *The Great Cryptogram : Francis Bacon's Cipher in the* so-called Shakspere Plays. With facsimiles. 2 vols., 30s.

Donkin (J. G.) Trooper and Redskin : N.W. Mounted Police, Canada. Crown 8vo, 8s. 6d.

Dougall (James Dalziel) Shooting: its Appliances, Practice, and Purpose. New Edition, revised with additions. Crown 8vo, 7s. 6d.

"The book is admirable in every way. . . . . We wish it every success."—*Globe.*

"A very complete treatise. . . . . Likely to take high rank as an authority on shooting."—*Daily News.*

Doughty (H.M.) Friesland Meres, and through the Netherlands.
Illustrated, crown 8vo, 8*s.* 6*d.*
Dramatic Year: Brief Criticisms of Events in the U.S. By W.
ARCHER. Crown 8vo, 6*s.*
Dunstan Standard Readers. Ed. by A. GILL, of Cheltenham.

*E*ARL *(H. P.) Randall Trevor.* 2 vols., crown 8vo, 21*s.*

Eastwood (F.) In Satan's Bonds. 2 vols., crown 8vo, 21*s.*
Edmonds (C.) Poetry of the Anti-Jacobin. With Additional
matter. New ed. Illust., crown 8vo, 7*s.* 6*d.* ; large paper, 21*s.*
Educational List and Directory for 1887-88. 5*s.*
Educational Works published in Great Britain. A Classi-
fied Catalogue. Third Edition. 8vo, cloth extra, 6*s.*
Edwards (E.) American Steam Engineer. Illust., 12mo, 12*s.* 6*d.*
Eight Months on the Argentine Gran Chaco. 8vo, 8*s.* 6*d.*
Elliott (H. W.) An Arctic Province : Alaska and the Seal
Islands. Illustrated from Drawings ; also with Maps. 16*s.*
Emerson (Dr. P. H.) English Idylls. Small post 8vo, 2*s.*
———— *Pictures of East Anglian Life.* Ordinary edit., 105*s.* ;
édit. de luxe, 17 × 13½, vellum, morocco back, 147*s.*
———— *Naturalistic Photography for Art Students.* Illustrated.
New edit. 5*s.*
———— *and Goodall. Life and Landscape on the Norfolk*
Broads. Plates 12 × 8 inches, 126*s.*; large paper, 210*s.*
Emerson in Concord : A Memoir written by Edward Waldo
EMERSON. 8vo, 7*s.* 6*d.*
English Catalogue of Books. Vol. III., 1872—1880. Royal
8vo, half-morocco, 42*s.* See also " Index."
English Etchings. Published Quarterly. 3*s.* 6*d.* Vol. VI., 25*s.*
English Philosophers. Edited by E. B. IVAN MÜLLER, M.A.
Crown 8vo volumes of 180 or 200 pp., price 3*s.* 6*d.* each.

Francis Bacon, by Thomas Fowler. | Shaftesbury and Hutcheson.
Hamilton, by W. H. S. Monck. | Adam Smith, by J. A. Farrer.
Hartley and James Mill. |

Esmarch (F.) Handbook of Surgery. Translation from the
last German Edition. With 647 new Illustrations. 8vo, leather, 24*s.*
Eton. About some Fellows. New Edition, 1*s.*
Evelyn. Life of Mrs. Godolphin. By WILLIAM HARCOURT,
of Nuneham. Steel Portrait. Extra binding, gilt top, 7*s.* 6*d.*
· *Eves (C. W.) West Indies.* (Royal Colonial Institute publica-
tion.) Crown 8vo, 7*s.* 6*d.*

*F*ARINI *(G. A.) Through the Kalahari Desert.* 8vo, 21*s.*

Farm Ballads, Festivals, and Legends. See CARLETON.

Fay (T.) Three Germanys ; glimpses into their History. 2 vols., 8vo, 35*s*.

Fenn (G. Manville) Off to the Wilds: a Story for Boys. Profusely Illustrated. Crown 8vo, gilt edges, 3*s*. 6*d*.; plainer, 2*s*. 6*d*.

———— *Silver Cañon.* Illust., gilt ed., 3*s*. 6*d*. ; plainer, 2*s*. 6*d*.

Fennell (Greville) Book of the Roach. New Edition, 12mo, 2*s*.

Ferns. See HEATH.

Fitzgerald (P.) Book Fancier. Cr. 8vo. 5*s*. ; large pap. 12*s*. 6*d*.

Fleming (Sandford) England and Canada : a Tour. Cr. 8vo, 6*s*.

Florence. See YRIARTE.

Folkard (R., Jun.) Plant Lore, Legends, and Lyrics. 8vo, 16*s*.

Forbes (H. O.) Naturalist in the Eastern Archipelago. 8vo. 21*s*.

Foreign Countries and British Colonies. Cr. 8vo, 3*s*. 6*d*. each.

Australia, by J. F. Vesey Fitzgerald.
Austria, by D. Kay, F.R.G.S.
Denmark and Iceland, by E. C. Otté.
Egypt, by S. Lane Poole, B.A.
France, by Miss M. Roberts.
Germany, by S. Baring-Gould.
Greece, by L. Sergeant, B.A.
Japan, by S. Mossman.
Peru, by Clements R. Markham.
Russia, by W. R. Morfill, M.A.
Spain, by Rev. Wentworth Webster.
Sweden and Norway, by Woods.
West Indies, by C. H. Eden, F.R.G.S.

Franc (Maud Jeanne). Small post 8vo, uniform, gilt edges :—

Emily's Choice. 5*s*.
Hall's Vineyard. 4*s*.
John's Wife : A Story of Life in South Australia. 4*s*.
Marian ; or, The Light of Some One's Home. 5*s*.
Silken Cords and Iron Fetters. 4*s*.
Into the Light. 4*s*.
Vermont Vale. 5*s*.
Minnie's Mission. 4*s*.
Little Mercy. 4*s*.
Beatrice Melton's Discipline. 4*s*.
No Longer a Child. 4*s*.
Golden Gifts. 4*s*.
Two Sides to Every Question. 4*s*.
Master of Ralston. 4*s*.

*** There is also a re-issue in cheaper form at 2*s*. 6*d*. per vol.

Frank's Ranche ; or, My Holiday in the Rockies. A Contribution to the Inquiry into What we are to Do with our Boys. 5*s*.

Fraser (Bishop). See DIGGLE.

French. See JULIEN and PORCHER.

Fresh Woods and Pastures New. By the Author of "An Amateur Angler's Days." 1*s*. 6*d*.; large paper, 5*s*. ; new ed., 1*s*.

Froissart. See LANIER.

Fuller (Edward) Fellow Travellers. 3*s*. 6*d*.

———— See also "Dramatic Year."

GASPARIN (Countess A. de) Sunny Fields and Shady Woods. 6*s*.

Geary (Grattan) Burma after the Conquest. 7*s*. 6*d*.

Geffcken (F. H.) British Empire. Translated by S. J. MACMULLAN. Crown 8vo, 7*s*. 6*d*.

Gentle Life (Queen Edition).   2 vols. in 1, small 4to, 6*s.*

THE GENTLE LIFE SERIES.

**Price 6*s.* each ; or in calf extra, price 10*s.* 6*d.* ; Smaller Edition, cloth
extra, 2*s.* 6*d.*, except where price is named.**

The Gentle Life.   Essays in aid of the Formation of Character.
About in the World.   Essays by Author of " The Gentle Life."
Like unto Christ.   New Translation of Thomas à Kempis.
Familiar Words.   A Quotation Handbook.   6*s.*; n. ed. 3*s.*6*d.*
Essays by Montaigne.   Edited by the Author of " The Gentle
   Life."
The Gentle Life.   2nd Series.
The Silent Hour : Essays, Original and Selected.
Half-Length Portraits.   Short Studies of Notable Persons.
   By J. HAIN FRISWELL.
Essays on English Writers, for Students in English Literature.
Other People's Windows.   By J. HAIN FRISWELL.   6*s.* ; new
   ed., 3*s.* 6*d.*
A Man's Thoughts.   By J. HAIN FRISWELL.
Countess of Pembroke's Arcadia.   By Sir P. SIDNEY.   6*s.*; new
   ed., 3*s.* 6*d.*

Germany.   By S. BARING-GOULD.   Crown 8vo, 3*s.* 6*d.*
Gibbon (C.) Beyond Compare : a Story.   3 vols., cr. 8vo, 31*s.* 6*d.*
Giles (E.) Australia twice Traversed : five Expeditions, 1872-76.
   With Maps and Illust. 2 vols, 8vo, 30*s.*
Gillespie (W. M.) Surveying.   Revised and enlarged by CADEY
   STALEY.   8vo, 21*s.*
Goethe.   Faustus.   Translated in the original rhyme and metre
   by A. H. HUTH.   Crown 8vo, 5*s.*
Goldsmith.   She Stoops to Conquer.   Introduction by AUSTIN
   DOBSON ; the designs by E. A. ABBEY.   Imperial 4to, 42*s.*
Gordon (J. E. H., B.A. Cantab.) Electric Lighting.   Ill. 8vo, 18*s.*
   —— *Physical Treatise on Electricity and Magnetism.*   2nd
   Edition, enlarged, with coloured, full-page, &c., Illust. 2 vols., 8vo, 42*s.*
   —— *Electricity for Schools.*   Illustrated.   Crown 8vo, 5*s.*
Gouffé (Jules) Royal Cookery Book.   New Edition, with plates
   in colours, Woodcuts, &c., 8vo, gilt edges, 42*s.*
   —— Domestic Edition, half-bound, 10*s.* 6*d.*
Grant (General, U.S.) Personal Memoirs.   With Illustrations
   Maps, &c.   2 vols., 8vo, 28*s.*
Great Artists.   See " Biographies."

Great Musicians. Edited by F. HUEFFER. A Series of
Biographies, crown 8vo, 3*s.* each :—

Bach.	Handel.	Rossini.
Beethoven.	Haydn.	Schubert.
Berlioz.	Mendelssohn.	Schumann.
English Church Com-posers. By BARRETT.	Mozart. Purcell.	Richard Wagner. Weber.

Groves (J. Percy) Charmouth Grange. Gilt, 5*s.*; plainer, 2*s.* 6*d.*

Guizot's History of France. Translated by R. BLACK. In
8 vols., super-royal 8vo, cloth extra, gilt, each 24*s.* In cheaper
binding, 8 vols., at 10*s.* 6*d.* each.

 " It supplies a want which has long been felt, and ought to be in the hands of all
 students of history."—*Times.*

——————————————— *Masson's School Edition.* Abridged
from the Translation by Robert Black, with Chronological Index, His-
torical and Genealogical Tables, &c. By Professor GUSTAVE MASSON,
B.A. With Portraits, Illustrations, &c. 1 vol., 8vo, 600 pp., 5*s.*

Guyon (Mde.) Life. By UPHAM. 6th Edition, crown 8vo, 6*s.*

*H*ALFORD *(F. M.) Floating Flies, and how to Dress them.*
New edit., with Coloured plates. 8vo, 15*s.*

—— *Dry Fly-Fishing, Theory and Practice.* Col. Plates, 25*s.*

Hall (W. W.) How to Live Long; or, 1408 *Maxims.* 2*s.*

Hamilton (E.) Fly-fishing for Salmon, Trout, and Grayling ;
their Habits, Haunts, and History. Illust., 6*s.*; large paper, 10*s.* 6*d.*

Hands (T.) Numerical Exercises in Chemistry. Cr. 8vo, 2*s.* 6*d.*
and 2*s.*; Answers separately, 6*d.*

Hardy (A. S.) Passe-rose : a Romance. Crown 8vo, 6*s.*

Hardy (Thomas). See " Low's Standard Novels."

Hare (J. L. Clark) American Constitutional Law. 2 vls., 8vo, 63*s.*

Harper's Magazine. Monthly. 160 pages, fully illustrated, 1*s.*
Vols., half yearly, I.—XVIII., super-royal 8vo, 8*s.* 6*d.* each.

 " ' Harper's Magazine ' is so thickly sown with excellent illustrations that to coun
 them would be a work of time ; not that it is a picture magazine, for the engravings
 illustrate the text after the manner seen in some of our choicest *éditions de luxe.*"—
 St. James's Gazette.

 " It is so pretty, so big, and so cheap. . . . An extraordinary shillingsworth—
 160 large octavo pages, with over a score of articles, and more than three times as
 many illustrations."—*Edinburgh Daily Review.*

 " An amazing shillingsworth . . . combining choice literature of both nations."—
 Nonconformist.

Harper's Young People. Vols. I.-V., profusely Illustrated
with woodcuts and coloured plates. Royal 4to, extra binding, each
7*s.* 6*d.*; gilt edges, 8*s.* Published Weekly, in wrapper, 1*d.* ; Annual
Subscription, post free, 6*s.* 6*d.* ; Monthly, in wrapper, with coloured
plate, 6*d.* ; Annual Subscription, post free, 7*s.* 6*d.*

Harris (Bishop of Michigan) Dignity of Man : Select Sermons.
Crown 8vo, 8*s.* 6*d.*

Harris (W. B.) Land of African Sultan : Travels in Morocco.
Illust., crown 8vo, 10*s.* 6*d.* ; large paper, 31*s.* 6*d.*

Harrison (Mary) Complete Cookery Book. Crown 8vo.

———— *Skilful Cook.* New edition, crown 8vo, 5s.

Harrison (W.) Memorable London Houses : a Guide. Illust. New edition, 18mo, 1s. 6d.

Hatton (Joseph) Journalistic London : with Engravings and Portraits of Distinguished Writers of the Day. Fcap. 4to, 12s. 6d.

———— See also LOW'S STANDARD NOVELS.

Haweis (Mrs.) Art of Housekeeping : a Bridal Garland. 2s. 6d.

Hawthorne (Nathaniel) Life. By JOHN R. LOWELL.

Heldmann (B.) Mutiny of the Ship "Leander." Gilt edges, 3s. 6d.; plainer, 2s. 6d.

Henty. Winning his Spurs. Cr. 8vo, 3s. 6d. ; plainer, 2s. 6d.

———— *Cornet of Horse.* Cr. 8vo, 3s. 6d.; plainer, 2s. 6d.

———— *Jack Archer.* Illust. 3s. 6d. ; plainer, 2s. 6d.

Henty (Richmond) Australiana : My Early Life. 5s.

Herrick (Robert) Poetry. Preface by AUSTIN DOBSON. With numerous Illustrations by E. A. ABBEY. 4to, gilt edges, 42s.

Hetley (Mrs. E.) Native Flowers of New Zealand. Chromos from Drawings. Three Parts, 63s.; extra binding, 73s. 6d.

Hicks (E. S.) Our Boys: How to Enter the Merchant Service. 5s.

———— *Yachts, Boats and Canoes.* Illustrated. 8vo, 10s. 6d.

Hinman (R.) Eclectic Physical Geography. Crown 8vo, 5s.

Hitchman. Public Life of the Earl of Beaconsfield. 3s. 6d.

Hoey (Mrs. Cashel) See LOW'S STANDARD NOVELS.

Holder (C. F.) Marvels of Animal Life. Illustrated. 8s. 6d.

———— *Ivory King : Elephant and Allies.* Illustrated. 8s. 6d.

———— *Living Lights : Phosphorescent Animals and Vegetables.* Illustrated. 8vo, 8s. 6d.

Holmes (O. W.) Before the Curfew, &c. Occasional Poems. 5s.

———— *Last Leaf : a Holiday Volume.* 42s.

———— *Mortal Antipathy*, 8s. 6d. ; also 2s. ; paper, 1s.

———— *Our Hundred Days in Europe.* 6s. Large Paper, 15s.

———— *Poetical Works.* 2 vols., 18mo, gilt tops, 10s. 6d.

———— See also "Rose Library."

Howard (Blanche Willis) Open Door. Crown 8vo, 6s.

Howorth (H. H.) Mammoth and the Flood. 8vo, 18s.

Hugo (V.) Notre Dame. With coloured etchings and 150 engravings. 2 vols., 8vo, vellum cloth, 30s.

Hundred Greatest Men (The). 8 portfolios, 21s. each, or 4 vols., half-morocco, gilt edges, 10 guineas. New Ed., 1 vol., royal 8vo, 21s.

Hymnal Companion to the Book of Common Prayer. By BISHOP BICKERSTETH. In various styles and bindings from 1d. to 31s. 6d. *Price List and Prospectus will be forwarded on application.*

ILLUSTRATED Text-Books of Art-Education. Edited by EDWARD J. POYNTER, R.A. Illustrated, and strongly bound, 5*s.* Now ready:—

PAINTING.

Classic and Italian. By HEAD. | French and Spanish.
German, Flemish, and Dutch. | English and American.

ARCHITECTURE.

Classic and Early Christian.
Gothic and Renaissance. By T. ROGER SMITH.

SCULPTURE.

Antique: Egyptian and Greek.
Renaissance and Modern. By LEADER SCOTT.

Inderwick (F. A.; Q.C.) Side Lights on the Stuarts. Essays. Illustrated, 8vo, 18*s.*

Index to the English Catalogue, Jan., 1874, *to Dec.,* 1880. Royal 8vo, half-morocco, 18*s.*

Inglis (Hon. James; "Maori") Our New Zealand Cousins. Small post 8vo, 6*s.*

———— *Tent Life in Tiger Land: Twelve Years a Pioneer* Planter. Col. plates, roy. 8vo, 18*s.*

Irving (Washington). Library Edition of his Works in 27 vols., Copyright, with the Author's Latest Revisions. "Geoffrey Crayon" Edition, large square 8vo. 12*s.* 6*d.* per vol. *See also* "Little Britain."

JACKSON. New Style Vertical Writing Copy-Books Series 1, Nos. I.—XII., 2*d.* and 1*d.* each.

———— *New Series of Vertical Writing Copy-books.* 22 Nos.

———— *Shorthand of Arithmetic: a Companion to all Arithmetics.* Crown 8vo, 1*s.* 6*d.*

Japan. See ANDERSON, ARTISTIC, AUDSLEY, also MORSE.

Jerdon (Gertrude) Key-hole Country. Illustrated. Crown 8vo, cloth, 2*s.*

Johnston (H. H.) River Congo, from its Mouth to Bolobo. New Edition, 8vo, 21*s.*

Johnstone (D. Lawson) Land of the Mountain Kingdom. Illust., crown 8vo. 5*s.*

Julien (F.) English Student's French Examiner. 16mo, 2*s.*

———— *Conversational French Reader.* 16mo, cloth, 2*s.* 6*d.*

————*French at Home and at School.* Book I., Accidence 2*s.*

———— *First Lessons in Conversational French Grammar.* 1*s.*

———— *Petites Leçons de Conversation et de Grammaire.* 3*s.*

———— *Phrases of Daily Use.* Limp cloth, 6*d.*

KARR (H. W. Seton) Shores and Alps of Alaska. 8vo, 16*s.*

Keats. Endymion. Illust. by W. ST. JOHN HARPER. Imp. 4to, gilt top, 42*s.*

Kempis (Thomas à) Daily Text-Book. Square 16mo, 2s. 6d.;
interleaved as a Birthday Book, 3s. 6d.

Kennedy (E. B.) Blacks and Bushrangers, adventures in North
Queensland. Illust., crown 8vo, 7s. 6d.

Kent's Commentaries ; an Abridgment for Students of American
Law. By EDEN F. THOMPSON. 10s. 6d.

Kerr (W. M.) Far Interior : Cape of Good Hope, across the
Zambesi, to the Lake Regions. Illustrated from Sketches, 2 vols.
8vo, 32s.

Kershaw (S. W.) Protestants from France in their English
Home. Crown 8vo, 6s.

King (Henry) Savage London ; Riverside Characters, &c.
Crown 8vo, 6s.

Kingston (W. H. G.) Works. Illustrated, 16mo, gilt edges,
3s. 6d.; plainer binding, plain edges, 2s. 6d. each.

Ben Burton.	Heir of Kilfinnan.
Captain Mugford, or, Oar Salt	Snow-Shoes and Canoes.
and Fresh Water Tutors.	Two Supercargoes.
Dick Cheveley.	With Axe and Rifle.

Kingsley (Rose) Children of Westminster Abbey : Studies in
English History. 5s.

Knight (E. J.) Cruise of the " Falcon." New Ed. Cr. 8vo,
7s. 6d.

Knox (Col.) Boy Travellers on the Congo. Illus. Cr. 8vo, 7s. 6d.

Kunhardt (C. B.) Small Yachts : Design and Construction. 35s.

—— *Steam Yachts and Launches.* Illustrated. 4to, 16s.

LANGLEY (S. P.) New Astronomy. Ill. Cr. 8vo. 10s. 6d.

Lanier's Works. Illustrated, crown 8vo, gilt edges, 7s. 6d.
each.

Boy's King Arthur.	Boy's Percy: Ballads of Love and
Boy's Froissart.	Adventure, selected from the
Boy's Knightly Legends of Wales.	" Reliques."

Lansdell (H.) Through Siberia. 2 vols., 8vo, 30s.; 1 vol., 10s. 6d.

—— *Russia in Central Asia.* Illustrated. 2 vols., 42s.

—— *Through Central Asia ; Russo-Afghan Frontier, &c.*
8vo, 12s.

Larden (W.) School Course on Heat. Third Ed., Illust. 5s.

Laurie (A.) Conquest of the Moon : a Story of the Bayouda.
Illust., crown 8vo, 7s. 6d.

Layard (Mrs. Granville) Through the West Indies. Small
post 8vo, 2s. 6d.

Lea (H. C.). History of the Inquisition of the Middle Ages.
3 vols., 8vo, 42s.

Lemon (M.) Small House over the Water, and Stories. Illust. by Cruikshank, &c. Crown 8vo, 6s.

Leo XIII.: Life. By BERNARD O'REILLY. With Steel Portrait from Photograph, &c. Large 8vo, 18s.; *édit. de luxe*, 63s.

Leonardo da Vinci's Literary Works. Edited by Dr. JEAN PAUL RICHTER. Containing his Writings on Painting, Sculpture, and Architecture, his Philosophical Maxims, Humorous Writings, and Miscellaneous Notes on Personal Events, on his Contemporaries, on Literature, &c.; published from Manuscripts. 2 vols., imperial 8vo, containing about 200 Drawings in Autotype Reproductions, and numerous other Illustrations. Twelve Guineas.

Library of Religious Poetry. Best Poems of all Ages. Edited by SCHAFF and GILMAN. Royal 8vo, 21s.; cheaper binding, 10s. 6d.

Lindsay (W. S.) History of Merchant Shipping. Over 150 Illustrations, Maps, and Charts. In 4 vols., demy 8vo, cloth extra. Vols. 1 and 2, 11s. each; vols. 3 and 4, 14s. each. 4 vols., 50s.

Little (Archibald J.) Through the Yang-tse Gorges: Trade and Travel in Western China. New Edition. 8vo, 10s. 6d.

Little Britain, The Spectre Bridegroom, and *Legend of Sleepy* Hollow. By WASHINGTON IRVING. An entirely New *Édition de luxe.* Illustrated by 120 very fine Engravings on Wood, by Mr. J. D. COOPER. Designed by Mr. CHARLES O. MURRAY. Re-issue, square crown 8vo, cloth, 6s.

Lodge (Henry Cabot) George Washington. (American Statesmen.) 2 vols., 12s.

Longfellow. Maidenhood. With Coloured Plates. Oblong 4to, 2s. 6d.; gilt edges, 3s. 6d.

—— *Courtship of Miles Standish.* Illust. by BROUGHTON, &c. Imp. 4to, 21s.

—— *Nuremberg.* 28 Photogravures. Illum. by M. and A. COMEGYS. 4to, 31s. 6d.

Lowell (J. R.) Vision of Sir Launfal. Illustrated, royal 4to, 63s.

—— *Life of Nathaniel Hawthorne.* Sm post 8vo. [*In prep.*

Low's Standard Library of Travel and Adventure. Crown 8vo, uniform in cloth extra, 7s. 6d., except where price is given.

1. **The Great Lone Land.** By Major W. F. BUTLER, C.B.
2. **The Wild North Land.** By Major W. F. BUTLER, C.B.
3. **How I found Livingstone.** By H. M. STANLEY.
4. **Through the Dark Continent.** By H. M. STANLEY. 12s. 6d.
5. **The Threshold of the Unknown Region.** By C. R. MARKHAM. (4th Edition, with Additional Chapters, 10s. 6d.)
6. **Cruise of the Challenger.** By W. J. J. SPRY, R.N.
7. **Burnaby's On Horseback through Asia Minor.** 10s. 6d.
8. **Schweinfurth's Heart of Africa.** 2 vols., 15s.
9. **Through America.** By W. G. MARSHALL.
10. **Through Siberia.** Il. and unabridged, 10s. 6d. By H. LANSDELL.
11. **From Home to Home.** By STAVELEY HILL.
12. **Cruise of the Falcon.** By E. J. KNIGHT.

Low's Standard Library, &c.—continued.
13. **Through Masai Land.** By JOSEPH THOMSON.
, 14. **To the Central African Lakes.** By JOSEPH THOMSON.
15. **Queen's Highway.** By STUART CUMBERLAND.

Low's Standard Novels. Small post 8vo, cloth extra, 6s. each, unless otherwise stated

JAMES BAKER. **John Westacott.**
WILLIAM BLACK.
  A Daughter of Heth.—House-Boat.—In Far Lochaber.—In Silk Attire.—Kilmeny.—Lady Silverdale's Sweetheart.—Sunrise.—Three Feathers.
R. D. BLACKMORE.
  Alice Lorraine.—Christowell, a Dartmoor Tale.—Clara Vaughan.—Cradock Nowell.—Cripps the Carrier.—Erema; or, My Father's Sin.—Lorna Doone.—Mary Anerley.—Tommy Upmore.
G. W. CABLE. **Bonaventure.** 5s.
Miss COLERIDGE. **An English Squire.**
C. E. CRADDOCK. **Despot of Broomsedge Cove.**
Mrs. B. M. CROKER. **Some One Else.**
STUART CUMBERLAND. **Vasty Deep.**
E. DE LEON. **Under the Stars and Crescent.**
Miss BETHAM-EDWARDS. **Halfway.**
Rev. E. GILLIAT, M.A. **Story of the Dragonnades.**
THOMAS HARDY.
  A Laodicean.—Far from the Madding Crowd.—Mayor of Casterbridge.—Pair of Blue Eyes.—Return of the Native.—The Hand of Ethelberta.—The Trumpet Major.—Two on a Tower.
JOSEPH HATTON. **Old House at Sandwich.—Three Recruits.**
Mrs. CASHEL HOEY.
  A Golden Sorrow.—A Stern Chase.—Out of Court.
BLANCHE WILLIS HOWARD. **Open Door.**
JEAN INGELOW.
  Don John.—John Jerome (5s.).—Sarah de Berenger.
GEORGE MAC DONALD.
  Adela Cathcart.—Guild Court.—Mary Marston.—Stephen Archer (New Ed. of "Gifts").—The Vicar's Daughter.—Orts.—Weighed and Wanting.
Mrs. MACQUOID. **Diane.—Elinor Dryden.**
HELEN MATHERS. **My Lady Greensleeves.**
DUFFIELD OSBORNE. **Spell of Ashtaroth (5s.)**
Mrs. J. H. RIDDELL.
  Alaric Spenceley.—Daisies and Buttercups.—The Senior Partner.—A Struggle for Fame.
W. CLARK RUSSELL.
  Frozen Pirate.—Jack's Courtship.—John Holdsworth.—A Sailor's Sweetheart.—Sea Queen.—Watch Below.—Strange Voyage.—Wreck of the Grosvenor.—The Lady Maud.—Little Loo.

Low's Standard Novels—continued.
FRANK R. STOCKTON.
   Bee-man of Orn.—The Late Mrs. Null.—Hundredth Man.
Mrs. HARRIET B. STOWE.
   My Wife and I.—Old Town Folk.—We and our Neighbours.—
      Poganuc People, their Loves and Lives.
JOSEPH THOMSON.   Ulu: an African Romance.
LEW. WALLACE.   Ben Hur: a Tale of the Christ.
CONSTANCE FENIMORE WOOLSON.
   Anne.—East Angels.—For the Major (5s.).
French Heiress in her own Chateau.

See also SEA STORIES.

Low's Standard Novels.   NEW ISSUE at short intervals.   Cr.
   8vo, 2s. 6d.; fancy boards, 2s.
   BLACKMORE.
   Clara Vaughan.—Cripps the Carrier.—Lorna Doone.—Mary
      Anerley.
   HARDY.
   Madding Crowd.—Mayor of Casterbridge.—Trumpet-Major.
   HATTON.   Three Recruits.
   HOLMES.   Guardian Angel.
   MAC DONALD.   Adela Cathcart.—Guild Court.
   RIDDELL.   Daisies and Buttercups.—Senior Partner.
   STOCKTON.   Casting Away of Mrs. Lecks.
   STOWE.   Dred.
   WALFORD.   Her Great Idea.

To be followed immediately by

BLACKMORE.   Alice Lorraine.—Tommy Upmore.
CABLE.   Bonaventure.
CROKER.   Some One Else.
DE LEON.   Under the Stars.
EDWARDS.   Half-Way.
HARDY.
   Hand of Ethelberta.—Pair of Blue Eyes.—Two on a Tower.
HATTON.   Old House at Sandwich.
HOEY.   Golden Sorrow.—Out of Court.—Stern Chase.
INGELOW.   John Jerome.—Sarah de Berenger.
MAC DONALD.   Vicar's Daughter.—Stephen Archer.
OLIPHANT.   Innocent.
STOCKTON.   Bee-Man of Orn.
STOWE.   Old Town Folk.—Poganuc People.
THOMSON.   Ulu.

Low's Standard Books for Boys.   With numerous Illustrations,
   2s. 6d.; gilt edges, 3s. 6d. each.
   Dick Cheveley.   By W. H. G. KINGSTON.
   Heir of Kilfinnan.   By W. H. G. KINGSTON.
   Off to the Wilds.   By G. MANVILLE FENN.
   The Two Supercargoes.   By W. H. G. KINGSTON.
   The Silver Cañon.   By G. MANVILLE FENN.
   Under the Meteor Flag.   By HARRY COLLINGWOOD.
   Jack Archer: a Tale of the Crimea.   By G. A. HENTY.

Low's Standard Books for Boys—continued.

The Mutiny on Board the Ship Leander. By B. HELDMANN.
With Axe and Rifle on the Western Prairies. By W. H. G. KINGSTON.
Red Cloud, the Solitary Sioux: a Tale of the Great Prairie. By Col. Sir WM. BUTLER, K.C.B.
The Voyage of the Aurora. By HARRY COLLINGWOOD.
Charmouth Grange: a Tale of the 17th Century. By J. PERCY GROVES.
Snowshoes and Canoes. By W. H. G. KINGSTON.
The Son of the Constable of France. By LOUIS ROUSSELET.
Captain Mugford; or, Our Salt and Fresh Water Tutors. Edited by W. H. G. KINGSTON.
The Cornet of Horse, a Tale of Marlborough's Wars. By G. A. HENTY.
The Adventures of Captain Mago. By LEON CAHUN.
Noble Words and Noble Needs.
The King of the Tigers. By ROUSSELET.
Hans Brinker; or, The Silver Skates. By Mrs. DODGE.
The Drummer-Boy, a Story of the time of Washington. By ROUSSELET.
Adventures in New Guinea: The Narrative of Louis Tregance.
The Crusoes of Guiana. By BOUSSENARD.
The Gold Seekers. A Sequel to the Above. By BOUSSENARD.
Winning His Spurs, a Tale of the Crusades. By G. A. HENTY.
The Blue Banner. By LEON CAHUN.

New Volumes for 1889.

Startling Exploits of the Doctor. CÉLIÈRE.
Brothers Rantzau. ERCKMANN-CHATRIAN.
Young Naturalist. BIART.
Ben Burton; or, Born and Bred at Sea. KINGSTON.
Great Hunting Grounds of the World. MEUNIER.
Ran Away from the Dutch. PERELAER.
My Kalulu, Prince, King, and Slave. STANLEY.

Low's Standard Series of Books by Popular Writers. Sm. cr. 8vo, cloth gilt, 2*s.*; gilt edges, 2*s.* 6*d.* each.

Aunt Jo's Scrap Bag. By Miss ALCOTT.
Shawl Straps. By Miss ALCOTT.
Little Men. By Miss ALCOTT.
Hitherto. By Mrs. WHITNEY.
Forecastle to Cabin. By SAMUELS. Illustrated.
In My Indian Garden. By PHIL ROBINSON.
Little Women and Little Women Wedded. By Miss ALCOTT.
Eric and Ethel. By FRANCIS FRANCIS. Illust.
Keyhole Country. By GERTRUDE JERDON. Illust.
We Girls. By Mrs. WHITNEY.
The Other Girls. A Sequel to "We Girls." By Mrs. WHITNEY.
Adventures of Jimmy Brown. Illust. By W. L. ALDEN.
Under the Lilacs. By Miss ALCOTT. Illust.
Jimmy's Cruise. By Miss ALCOTT.
Under the Punkah. By PHIL ROBINSON.

Low's Standard Series of Books by Popular Writers—continued.
  An Old-Fashioned Girl. By Miss ALCOTT.
  A Rose in Bloom. By Miss ALCOTT.
  Eight Cousins. Illust. By Miss ALCOTT.
  Jack and Jill. By Miss ALCOTT.
  Lulu's Library. Illust. By Miss ALCOTT.
  Silver Pitchers. By Miss ALCOTT.
  Work and Beginning Again. Illust. By Miss ALCOTT.
  A Summer in Leslie Goldthwaite's Life. By Mrs. WHITNEY.
  Faith Gartney's Girlhood. By Mrs. WHITNEY.
  Real Folks. By Mrs. WHITNEY.
  Dred. By Mrs. STOWE.
  My Wife and I. By Mrs. STOWE.
  An Only Sister. By Madame DE WITT.
  Spinning Wheel Stories. By Miss ALCOTT.
  My Summer in a Garden. By C. DUDLEY WARNER.

Low's Pocket Encyclopædia: a Compendium of General Know-
  ledge for Ready Reference. Upwards of 25,000 References, with
  Plates. New ed., imp. 32mo, cloth, marbled edges, 3s. 6d.; roan, 4s. 6d.

Low's Handbook to London Charities. Yearly, cloth, 1s. 6d.;
  paper, 1s.

Lusignan (Princess A. de) Twelve years' Reign of Abdul Hamid
  II. Crown 8vo, 7s. 6d.

MᶜCULLOCH (H.) *Men and Measures of Half a century.*
  Sketches and Comments. 8vo, 18s.

Macdonald (D.) Oceania. Linguistic and Anthropological.
  Illust., and Tables. Crown 8vo, 6s.

Mac Donald (George). See LOW'S STANDARD NOVELS.

Macgregor (John) "Rob Roy" on the Baltic. 3rd Edition,
  small post 8vo, 2s. 6d.; cloth, gilt edges, 3s. 6d.

—————— *A Thousand Miles in the "Rob Roy" Canoe.* 11th
  Edition, small post 8vo, 2s. 6d.; cloth, gilt edges, 3s. 6d.

—————— *Voyage Alone in the Yawl "Rob Roy."* New Edition,
  with additions, small post 8vo, 3s. 6d. and 2s. 6d.

Mackenzie (Sir Morell) Fatal Illness of Frederick the Noble.
  Crown 8vo, limp cloth, 2s. 6d.

Mackenzie (Rev. John) Austral Africa : Losing it or Ruling it ?
  Illustrations and Maps. 2 vols., 8vo, 32s.

Maclean (H. E.) Maid of the Golden Age. Illust., cr. 8vo, 6s.

McLellan's Own Story : The War for the Union. Illust. 18s.

Maginn (W.) Miscellanies. Prose and Verse. With Memoir.
  2 vols., crown 8vo, 24s.

Main (Mrs.; Mrs. Fred Burnaby) High Life and Towers of
  Silence. Illustrated, square 8vo, 10s. 6d.

Malan (C. F. de M.) Eric and Connie's Cruise in the South
  Pacific. Crown 8vo, 5s.

Manning (E. F.) Delightful Thames. Illustrated. 4to, fancy boards, 5*s*.

Markham (Clements R.) The Fighting Veres, Sir F. and Sir H. 8vo, 18*s*.

———— *War between Peru and Chili,* 1879-1881. Third Ed. Crown 8vo, with Maps, 10*s*. 6*d*.

———— See also "Foreign Countries," MAURY, and VERES.

Marston (W.) Eminent Recent Actors, Reminiscences Critical, &c. 2 vols. Crown 8vo, 21*s*.; new edit., 1 vol., 6*s*.

Martin (F. W.) Float Fishing and Spinning in the Nottingham Style. New Edition. Crown 8vo, 2*s*. 6*d*.

Matthews (J. W., M.D.) Incwadi Yami : Twenty years in South Africa. With many Engravings, royal 8vo, 14*s*.

Maury (Commander) Physical Geography of the Sea, and its Meteorology. New Edition, with Charts and Diagrams, cr. 8vo, 6*s*.

———— *Life.* By his Daughter. Edited by Mr. CLEMENTS R. MARKHAM. With portrait of Maury. 8vo, 12*s*. 6*d*.

Melio (G. L.) Manual of Swedish Drill for Teachers and Students. Cr. 8vo, 1*s*. 6*d*.

Men of Mark : Portraits of the most Eminent Men of the Day. Complete in 7 Vols., 4to, handsomely bound, gilt edges, 25*s*. each.

Mendelssohn Family (The), 1729—1847. From Letters and Journals. Translated. New Edition, 2 vols., 8vo, 30*s*.

Mendelssohn. See also " Great Musicians."

Merrifield's Nautical Astronomy. Crown 8vo, 7*s*. 6*d*.

Mills (J.) Alternative Elementary Chemistry. Ill., cr.8vo, 1*s*.6*d*.

Mitford (Mary Russell) Our Village. With 12 full-page and 157 smaller Cuts. Cr. 4to, cloth, gilt edges, 21*s*.; cheaper binding, 10*s*.6*d*.

Mody (Mrs.) Outlines of German Literature. 18mo, 1*s*.

Moffatt (W.) Land and Work ; Depression, Agricultural and Commercial. Crown 8vo, 5*s*.

Mohammed Benani : A Story of To-day. 8vo, 10*s*. 6*d*.

Mollett (J. W.) Illustrated Dictionary of Words used in Art and Archæology. Illustrated, small 4to, 15*s*.

Moore (J. M.) New Zealand for Emigrant, Invalid and Tourist. Cr. 8vo.

Morley (Henry) English Literature in the Reign of Victoria. 2000th volume of the Tauchnitz Collection of Authors. 18mo, 2*s*. 6*d*.

Mormonism. See STENHOUSE.

Morse (E. S.) Japanese Homes and their Surroundings. With more than 300 Illustrations. Re-issue, 10*s*. 6*d*.

Morten (Honnor) Sketches of Hospital Life. Cr. 8vo, sewed, 1*s*.

Morwood. Our Gipsies in City, Tent, and Van. 8vo, 18*s*.

Moss (F. J.) Through Atolls and Islands of the great South Sea. Illust., crown 8vo, 8*s*. 6*d*.

Moxon (Walter) Pilocereus Senilis. Fcap. 8vo, gilt top, 3s. 6d.
Muller (E.) Noble Words and Noble Deeds. Illustrated, gilt
edges, 3s. 6d. ; plainer binding, 2s. 6d.
Musgrave (Mrs.) Miriam. Crown 8vo, 6s.
Music. See " Great Musicians."

NETHERCOTE (C. B.) Pytchley Hunt. New Ed., cr. 8vo,
8s. 6d.
New Zealand. See BRADSHAW and WHITE (J.).
New Zealand Rulers and Statesmen. See GISBORNE.
Nicholls (J. H. Kerry) The King Country : Explorations in
New Zealand. Many Illustrations and Map. New Edition, 8vo, 21s.
Nordhoff (C.) California, for Health, Pleasure, and Residence.
New Edition, 8vo, with Maps and Illustrations, 12s. 6d.
Norman (C. B.) Corsairs of France. With Portraits. 8vo, 18s.
North (W. ; M.A.) Roman Fever : an Inquiry during three
years' residence. Illust., 8vo, 25s.
Northbrook Gallery. Edited by LORD RONALD GOWER. 36 Per-
manent Photographs. Imperial 4to, 63s.; large paper, 105s.
Nott (Major) Wild Animals Photographed and Described. 35s.
Nursery Playmates (Prince of). 217 Coloured Pictures for
Children by eminent Artists. Folio, in col. bds., 6s.; new ed., 2s. 6d.
Nursing Record. Yearly, 8s.; half-yearly, 4s. 6d.; quarterly,
2s. 6d ; weekly, 2d.

O'BRIEN (R. B.) Fifty Years of Concessions to Ireland.
With a Portrait of T. Drummond. Vol. I., 16s., II., 16s.
Orient Line Guide. New edition re-written; by W. J. LOFTIE.
Maps and Plans, 2s. 6d.
Orvis (C. F.) Fishing with the Fly. Illustrated. 8vo, 12s. 6d.
Osborne (Duffield) Spell of Ashtaroth. Crown 8vo, 5s.
Our Little Ones in Heaven. Edited by the Rev. H. ROBBINS.
With Frontispiece after Sir JOSHUA REYNOLDS. New Edition, 5s.

PALGRAVE (R. F. D.) Oliver Cromwell and his Protec-
torate. Crown 8vo.
Pall ser (Mrs.) A History of Lace. New Edition, with additional cuts and text. 8vo, 21s.
—————— *The China Collector's Pocket Companion.* With upwards of 1000 Illustrations of Marks and Monograms. Small 8vo, 5s.
Panton (J. E.) Homes of Taste. Hints on Furniture and Deco-
ration. Crown 8vo, 2s. 6d.
Parsons (James ; A.M.) Exposition of the Principles of Partner-
ship. 8vo, 31s. 6d.

Pennell (H. Cholmondeley) Sporting Fish of Great Britain
15*s.* ; large paper, 30*s.*
———— *Modern Improvements in Fishing-tackle.* Crown 8vo, 2*s.*
Perelaer (M. T. H.) Ran Away from the Dutch ; Borneo, &c.
Illustrated, square 8vo, 7*s.* 6*d* ; new ed., 2*s.* 6*d.*
Perry (J. J. M.) Edlingham Burglary, or Circumstantial Evi-
dence. Crown 8vo, 3*s.* 6*d.*
Phelps (Elizabeth Stuart) Struggle for Immortality. Cr. 8vo, 5*s.*
Phillips' Dictionary of Biographical Reference. New edition,
royal 8vo, 25*s.*
Philpot (H. J.) Diabetes Mellitus. Crown 8vo, 5*s.*
———— *Diet System.* Tables. I. Diabetes ; II. Gout ;
III. Dyspepsia ; IV. Corpulence. In cases, 1*s.* each.
Plunkett (Major G. T.) Primer of Orthographic Projection.
Elementary Solid Geometry. With Problems and Exercises. 2*s.* 6*d.*
Poe (E. A.) The Raven. Illustr. by DORÉ. Imperial folio, 63*s.*
Poems of the Inner Life. Chiefly Modern. Small 8vo, 5*s.*
Poetry of the Anti-Jacobin. New ed., by CHARLES EDMONDS.
Cr. 8vo, 7*s.* 6*d.*; large paper, 21*s.*
Porcher (A.) Juvenile French Plays. With Notes and a
Vocabulary. 18mo, 1*s.*
Porter (Admiral David D.) Naval History of Civil War.
Portraits, Plans, &c. 4to, 25*s.*
Portraits of Celebrated Race-horses of the Past and Present
Centuries. with Pedigrees and Performances. 4 vols., 4to, 126*s.*
Powles (L. D.) Land of the Pink Pearl: Life in the Bahamas.
8vo, 10*s.* 6*d.*
Poynter (Edward J., R.A.). See " Illustrated Text-books."
Prince Maskiloff: a Romance of Modern Oxford. By ROY
TELLET. Crown 8vo, 10*s.* 6*d.*
Prince of Nursery Playmates. Col. plates, new ed., 2*s.* 6*d.*
Pritt (T. E.) North Country Flies. Illustrated from the
Author's Drawings. 10*s.* 6*d.*
Publishers' Circular (The), and General Record of British and
Foreign Literature. Published on the 1st and 15th of every Month, 3*d.*
Pyle (Howard) Otto of the Silver Hand. Illustrated by the
Author. 8vo, 8*s.* 6*d.*

QUEEN'S Prime Ministers. A series. Edited by S. J. REID.
Cr. 8vo, 2*s.* 6*d.* per vol.

RAMBAUD. History of Russia. New Edition, Illustrated.
3 vols., 8vo, 21*s.*

Reber. History of Mediæval Art. Translated by CLARKE. 422 Illustrations and Glossary. 8vo, .

Redford (G.) Ancient Sculpture. New Ed. Crown 8vo, 10s. 6d.

Redgrave (G. R.) Century of Painters of the English School. Crown 8vo, 10s. 6d.

Reed (Sir E. J., M.P.) and Simpson. Modern Ships of War. Illust., royal 8vo, 10s. 6d.

Reed (Talbot B.) Sir Ludar: a Tale of the Days of good Queen Bess. Crown 8vo, 6s.

Remarkable Bindings in the British Museum. India paper, 94s. 6d. ; sewed 73s. 6d. and 63s.

Reminiscences of a Boyhood in the early part of the Century: a Story. Crown 8vo, 6s.

Ricci (J. H. de) Fisheries Dispute, and the Annexation of Canada. Crown 8vo, 6s.

Richards (W.) Aluminium: its History, Occurrence, &c. Illustrated, crown 8vo, 12s. 6d.

Richter (Dr. Jean Paul) Italian Art in the National Gallery. 4to. Illustrated. Cloth gilt, £2 2s.; half-morocco, uncut, £2 12s. 6d.

—— See also LEONARDO DA VINCI.

Riddell (Mrs. J. H.) See LOW'S STANDARD NOVELS.

Roberts (W.) Earlier History of English Bookselling. Crown 8vo, 7s. 6d.

Robertson (T. W.) Principal Dramatic Works, with Portraits in photogravure. 2 vols., 21s.

Robin Hood; Merry Adventures of. Written and illustrated by HOWARD PYLE. Imperial 8vo, 15s.

Robinson (Phil.) In my Indian Garden. New Edition, 16mo, limp cloth, 2s.

—— *Noah's Ark. Unnatural History.* Sm. post 8vo, 12s. 6d.

—— *Sinners and Saints: a Tour across the United States of* America, and Round them. Crown 8vo, 10s. 6d.

—— *Under the Punkah.* New Ed., cr. 8vo, limp cloth, 2s.

Rockstro (W. S.) History of Music. New Edition. 8vo, 14s.

Roe (E. P.) Nature's Serial Story. Illust. New ed. 3s. 6d.

Roland, The Story of. Crown 8vo, illustrated, 6s.

Rose (J.) Complete Practical Machinist. New Ed., 12mo, 12s. 6d.

—— *Key to Engines and Engine-running.* Crown 8vo, 8s. 6d.

—— *Mechanical Drawing.* Illustrated, small 4to, 16s.

—— *Modern Steam Engines.* Illustrated. 31s. 6d.

—— *Steam Boilers. Boiler Construction and Examination.* Illust., 8vo, 12s. 6d.

Rose Library.   Each volume, 1s.   Many are illustrated—
  Little Women. By Louisa M. Alcott.
  Little Women Wedded. Forming a Sequel to "Little Women.
  Little Women and Little Women Wedded. 1 vol., cloth gilt, 3s. 6d.
  Little Men. By L. M. Alcott. Double vol., 2s.; cloth gilt, 3s. 6d.
  An Old-Fashioned Girl. By Louisa M. Alcott. 2s.; cloth,
     3s. 6d.
  Work. A Story of Experience. By L. M. Alcott. 3s. 6d.; 2 vols.,
     1s. each.
  Stowe (Mrs. H. B.) The Pearl of Orr's Island.
  ———— **The Minister's Wooing.**
  ———— **We and our Neighbours.** 2s.; cloth gilt, 6s.
  ———— **My Wife and I.** 2s.
  Hans Brinker; or, the Silver Skates. By Mrs. Dodge. Also 2s. 6d.
  My Study Windows. By J. R. Lowell.
  The Guardian Angel. By Oliver Wendell Holmes. Cloth, 2s.
  My Summer in a Garden. By C. D. Warner.
  Dred. By Mrs. Beecher Stowe. 2s.; cloth gilt, 3s. 6d.
  City Ballads. New Ed. 16mo. By Will Carleton.
  Farm Ballads. By Will Carleton. ⎫
  Farm Festivals. By Will Carleton. ⎬ 1 vol., cl., gilt ed., 3s. 6d.
  Farm Legends. By Will Carleton. ⎭
  The Rose in Bloom. By L. M. Alcott. 2s.; cloth gilt, 3s. 6d.
  Eight Cousins. By L. M. Alcott. 2s.; cloth gilt, 3s. 6d.
  Under the Lilacs. By L. M. Alcott. 2s.; also 3s. 6d.
  Undiscovered Country. By W. D. Howells.
  Clients of Dr. Bernagius. By L. Biart. 2 parts.
  Silver Pitchers. By Louisa M. Alcott. Cloth, 3s. 6d.
  Jimmy's Cruise in the "Pinafore," and other Tales. By
     Louisa M. Alcott. 2s.; cloth gilt, 3s. 6d.
  Jack and Jill. By Louisa M. Alcott. 2s.; Illustrated, 5s.
  Hitherto. By the Author of the "Gayworthys." 2 vols., 1s. each;
     1 vol., cloth gilt, 3s. 6d.
  A Gentleman of Leisure. A Novel. By Edgar Fawcett. 1s.

See also Low's Standard Series.

Ross (Mars) and Stonehewer Cooper. Highlands of Cantabria;
  or, Three Days from England. Illustrations and Map, 8vo, 21s.
Rothschilds, the Financial Rulers of Nations. By John
  Reeves. Crown 8vo, 7s. 6d.
Rousselet (Louis) Son of the Constable of France. Small post
  8vo, numerous Illustrations, gilt edges, 3s. 6d.; plainer, 2s. 6d.
———— *King of the Tigers: a Story of Central India.* Illus-
  trated. Small post 8vo, gilt, 3s. 6d.; plainer, 2s. 6d.
———— *Drummer Boy.* Illustrated. Small post 8vo, gilt
  edges, 3s. 6d.; plainer, 2s. 6d.
Russell (Dora) Strange Message. 3 vols., crown 8vo, 31s. 6d.
Russell (W. Clark) Betwixt the Forelands. Illust., crown 8vo,
  10s. 6d.

Russell (W. Clark) English Channel Ports and the Estate of the East and West India Dock Company. Crown 8vo, 1s.
—— *Sailor's Language.* Illustrated. Crown 8vo, 3s. 6d.
—— *Wreck of the Grosvenor.* 4to, sewed, 6d.
—— See also "Low's Standard Novels," "Sea Stories."

SAINTS and their Symbols: A Companion in the Churches and Picture Galleries of Europe. Illustrated. Royal 16mo, 3s. 6d.
Samuels (Capt. J. S.) From Forecastle to Cabin: Autobiography. Illustrated. Crown 8vo, 8s. 6d.; also with fewer Illustrations, cloth, 2s.; paper, 1s.
Saunders (A.) Our Domestic Birds: Poultry in England and New Zealand. Crown 8vo, 6s.
—— *Our Horses: the Best Muscles controlled by the Best* Brains. 6s.
Scherr (Prof. J.) History of English Literature. Cr. 8vo, 8s. 6d.
Schuyler (Eugène) American Diplomacy and the Furtherance of Commerce. 12s. 6d.
—— *The Life of Peter the Great.* 2 vols., 8vo, 32s.
Schweinfurth (Georg) Heart of Africa. 2 vols., crown 8vo, 15s.
Scott (Leader) Renaissance of Art in Italy. 4to, 31s. 6d.
—— *Sculpture, Renaissance and Modern.* 5s.
Sea Stories. By W. CLARK RUSSELL. New ed. Cr. 8vo, leather back, top edge gilt, per vol., 3s. 6d.

Frozen Pirate.	Sea Queen.
Jack's Courtship.	Strange Voyage.
John Holdsworth.	The Lady Maud.
Little Loo.	Watch Below.
Ocean Free Lance.	Wreck of the *Grosvenor.*
Sailor's Sweetheart.	

Semmes (Adm. Raphael) Service Afloat: The "Sumter" and the "Alabama." Illustrated. Royal 8vo, 16s.
Senior (W.) Near and Far: an Angler's Sketches of Home Sport and Colonial Life. Crown 8vo, 6s.; new edit., 2s.
—— *Waterside Sketches.* Imp. 32mo, 1s. 6d.; boards, 1s.
Shakespeare. Edited by R. GRANT WHITE. 3 vols., crown 8vo, gilt top, 36s.; *édition de luxe,* 6 vols., 8vo, cloth extra, 63s.
Shakespeare's Heroines: Studies by Living English Painters. 105s.; artists' proofs, 630s.
—— *Macbeth.* With Etchings on Copper, by J. MOYR SMITH. 105s. and 52s. 6d.
—— *Songs and Sonnets.* Illust. by Sir JOHN GILBERT, R.A. 4to, boards, 5s.
—— See also CUNDALL, DETHRONING, DONNELLY, MACKAY, and WHITE (R. GRANT).

Sharpe (R. Bowdler) Birds in Nature. 39 coloured plates and text. 4to, 63*s.*

Sheridan. Rivals. Reproductions of Water-colour, &c. 52*s.* 6*d.*; artists proofs, 105*s.* nett.

Shields (C. W.) Philosophia ultima ; from Harmony of Science and Religion. 2 vols. 8vo, 24*s.*

*Shields (G. O.) Cruisings in the Cascades; Hunting, Photo-*graphy, Fishing. 8vo, 10*s.* 6*d.*

Sidney (Sir Philip) Arcadia. New Edition, 3*s.* 6*d.*

Siegfried, The Story of. Illustrated, crown 8vo, cloth, 6*s.*

Simon. China : its Social Life. Crown 8vo, 6*s.*

Simson (A.) Wilds of Ecuador and Exploration of the Putumayor River. Crown 8vo, 8*s.* 6*d.*

Sinclair (Mrs.) Indigenous Flowers of the Hawaiian Islands. 44 Plates in Colour. Imp. folio, extra binding, gilt edges, 31*s.* 6*d.*

Sloane (T. O.) Home Experiments in Science for Old and Young. Crown 8vo, 6*s.*

Smith (G.) Assyrian Explorations. Illust. New Ed., 8vo, 18*s.*

———— *The Chaldean Account of Genesis.* With many Illustrations. 16*s.* New Ed. By Professor Sayce. 8vo, 18*s.*

Smith (G. Barnett) William I. and the German Empire. New Ed., 8vo, 3*s.* 6*d.*

Smith (Sydney) Life and Times. By Stuart J. Reid. Illustrated. 8vo, 21*s.*

Spiers' French Dictionary. 29th Edition, remodelled. 2 vols., 8vo, 18*s.*; half bound, 21*s.*

Spry (W. J. J., R.N., F.R.G.S.) Cruise of H.M.S." Challenger." With Illustrations. 8vo, 18*s.* Cheap Edit., crown 8vo, 7*s.* 6*d.*

Stanley (H. M.) Congo, and Founding its Free State. Illustrated, 2 vols., 8vo, 42*s.* ; re-issue, 2 vols. 8vo, 21*s.*

———— *How I Found Livingstone.* 8vo, 10*s.* 6*d.* ; cr. 8vo, 7*s.* 6*d.*

———— *Through the Dark Continent.* Crown 8vo, 12*s.* 6*d.*

Start (J. W. K.) Junior Mensuration Exercises. 8*d.*

Stenhouse (Mrs.) Tyranny of Mormonism. An Englishwoman in Utah. New ed., cr. 8vo, cloth elegant. 3*s.* 6*d.*

Sterry (J. Ashby) Cucumber Chronicles. 5*s.*

Stevens (E. W.) Fly-Fishing in Maine Lakes. 8*s.* 6*d.*

Stevens (T.) Around the World on a Bicycle. Vol. II. 8vo. 16*s.*

Stockton (Frank R.) Rudder Grange. 3*s.* 6*d.*

———— *Bee-Man of Orn, and other Fanciful Tales.* Cr. 8vo, 5*s.*

———— *Personally conducted.* Crown 8vo, 7*s.* 6*d.*

———— *The Casting Away of Mrs. Lecks and Mrs. Aleshine.* 1*s.*

———— *The Dusantes.* Sequel to the above. Sewed, 1*s.*; this and the preceding book in one volume, cloth, 2*s.* 6*d.*

Stockton (Frank R.) The Hundredth Man. Small post 8vo, 6s.
———— *The Late Mrs. Null.*   Small post 8vo, 6s.
———— *The Story of Viteau.*   Illust.   Cr. 8vo, 5s.
———— See also LOW'S STANDARD NOVELS.
Stowe (Mrs. Beecher) Dred. Cloth, gilt edges, 3s. 6d.; cloth, 2s.
———— *Flowers and Fruit from her Writings.*   Sm. post 8vo, 3s. 6d.
———— *Life, in her own Words . . . with Letters and Original* Compositions.   10s. 6d.
———— *Little Foxes.*   Cheap Ed., 1s.; Library Edition, 4s. 6d.
———— *My Wife and I.*   Cloth, 2s.
———— *Old Town Folk.*   6s.
———— *We and our Neighbours.*   2s.
———— *Poganuc People.*   6s.
———— See also ROSE LIBRARY.
Strachan (J.) Explorations and Adventures in New Guinea. Illust., crown 8vo, 12s.
Stranahan (C. H.) History of French Painting, the Academy, Salons, Schools, &c.   21s.
Stutfield (Hugh E. M.) El Maghreb: 1200 Miles' Ride through Marocco.   8s. 6d.
Sullivan (A. M.) Nutshell History of Ireland. Paper boards, 6d.
Sylvanus Redivivus, Rev. J. Mitford, with a Memoir of E. Jesse.   Crown 8vo, 10s. 6d.

TAINE (H. A.) "Origines."   Translated by JOHN DURAND.
  I.   **The Ancient Regime.**   Demy 8vo, cloth, 16s.
  II.   **The French Revolution.**   Vol. 1.   do.
  III.   **Do.**   do.   Vol. 2.   do.
  IV.   **Do.**   do.   Vol. 3.   do.
Tauchnitz's English Editions of German Authors.   Each volume, cloth flexible, 2s.; or sewed, 1s. 6d. (Catalogues post free.)
Tauchnitz (B.) German Dictionary.   2s.; paper, 1s. 6d.; roan, 2s. 6d.
———— *French Dictionary.*   2s.; paper, 1s. 6d.; roan, 2s. 6d.
———— *Italian Dictionary.*   2s.; paper, 1s. 6d.; roan, 2s. 6d.
———— *Latin Dictionary.*   2s.; paper, 1s. 6d.; roan, 2s. 6d.
———— *Spanish and English.*   2s.; paper, 1s. 6d.; roan, 2s. 6d.
———— *Spanish and French.*   2s.; paper, 1s. 6d.; roan, 2s. 6d.
Taylor (R. L.) Chemical Analysis Tables.   1s.
———— *Chemistry for Beginners.*   Small 8vo, 1s. 6d.
Techno-Chemical Receipt Book.   With additions by BRANNT and WAHL.   10s. 6d.

Technological Dictionary. See TOLHAUSEN.

Thausing (Prof.) Malt and the Fabrication of Beer. 8vo, 45*s.*

Theakston (M.) British Angling Flies. Illustrated. Cr. 8vo, 5*s.*

Thomson (Jos.) Central African Lakes. New edition, 2 vols. in one, crown 8vo, 7*s.* 6*d.*

—————— *Through Masai Land.* Illust. 21*s.*; new edition, 7*s.* 6*d.*

—————— *and Miss Harris-Smith. Ulu: an African Romance.* crown 8vo, 6*s.*

Thomson (W.) Algebra for Colleges and Schools. With Answers, 5*s.*; without, 4*s.* 6*d.*; Answers separate, 1*s.* 6*d.*

Thornton (L. D.) Story of a Poodle. By Himself and his Mistress. Illust., crown 4to, 2*s.* 6*d.*

Thorrodsen, Lad and Lass. Translated from the Icelandic by A. M. REEVES. Crown 8vo.

Tissandier (G.) Eiffel Tower. Illust., and letter of M. Eiffel in facsimile. Fcap. 8vo, 1*s.*

Tolhausen. Technological German, English, and French Dictionary. Vols. I., II., with Supplement, 12*s.* 6*d.* each; III., 9*s.*; Supplement, cr. 8vo, 3*s.* 6*d.*

Topmkins (E. S. de G.) Through David's Realm. Illust. by the Author. 8vo, 10*s.* 6*d.*

Tucker (W. J.) Life and Society in Eastern Europe. 15*s.*

Tuckerman (B.) Life of General Lafayette. 2 vols., cr. 8vo, 12*s.*

Tupper (Martin Farquhar) My Life as an Author. 14*s.*; new edition, 7*s.* 6*d.*

Tytler (Sarah) Duchess Frances: a Novel. 2 vols., 21*s.*

UPTON (H.) Manual of Practical Dairy Farming. Cr. 8vo, 2*s.*

VAN DAM. Land of Rubens; a companion for visitors to Belgium. Crown 8vo, 3*s.* 6*d.*

Vane (Young Sir Harry). By Prof. JAMES K. HOSMER. 8vo, 18*s.*

Veres. Biography of Sir Francis Vere and Lord Vere, leading Generals in the Netherlands. By CLEMENTS R. MARKHAM. 8vo, 18*s.*

Verne (Jules) Celebrated Travels and Travellers. 3 vols. 8vo, 7*s.* 6*d.* each; extra gilt, 9*s.*

Victoria (Queen) Life of. By GRACE GREENWOOD. Illust. 6*s.*

Vincent (Mrs. Howard) Forty Thousand Miles over Land and Water. With Illustrations. New Edit., 3*s.* 6*d.*

Viollet-le-Duc (E.) Lectures on Architecture. Translated by BENJAMIN BUCKNALL, Architect. 2 vols., super-royal 8vo, £3 3*s.*

BOOKS BY JULES VERNE.

WORKS.	In very handsome cloth binding, gilt edges.		In plainer binding, plain edges.		In cloth binding, gilt edges, smaller type.		Coloured boards, or cloth.
LARGE CROWN 8VO. — _Containing 350 to 600 pp. and from 50 to 100 full-page illustrations._					_Containing the whole of the text with some illustrations._		
	s.	d.	s.	d.	s.	d.	
20,000 Leagues under the Sea. Parts I. and II.	10	6	5	0	3	6	2 vols., 1s. each.
Hector Servadac	10	6	5	0	3	6	2 vols., 1s. each.
The Fur Country	10	6	5	0	3	6	2 vols., 1s. each.
The Earth to the Moon and a Trip round it	10	6	5	0	2 vols., 2s. ea.		2 vols., 1s. each.
Michael Strogoff	10	6	5	0	3	6	2 vols., 1s. each.
Dick Sands, the Boy Captain	10	6	5	0	3	6	2 vols., 1s. each.
Five Weeks in a Balloon	7	6	3	6	2	0	1s. 0d.
Adventures of Three Englishmen and Three Russians	7	6	3	6	2	0	1 0
Round the World in Eighty Days	7	6	3	6	2	0	1 0
A Floating City	7	6	3	6	2	0	1 0
The Blockade Runners					2	0	1 0
Dr. Ox's Experiment	—		—		2	0	1 0
A Winter amid the Ice	—		—		2	0	1 0
Survivors of the "Chancellor"	7	6	3	6	3	6	2 vols., 1s. each.
Martin Paz					2	0	1s. 0d.
The Mysterious Island, 3 vols.:—	22	6	10	6	6	0	3 0
I. Dropped from the Clouds	7	6	3	6	2	0	1 0
II. Abandoned	7	6	3	6	2	0	1 0
III. Secret of the Island	7	6	3	6	2	0	1 0
The Child of the Cavern	7	6	3	6	2	0	1 0
The Begum's Fortune	7	6	3	6	2	0	1 0
The Tribulations of a Chinaman	7	6	3	6	2	0	1 0
The Steam House, 2 vols.:—							
I. Demon of Cawnpore	7	6	3	6	2	0	1 0
II. Tigers and Traitors	7	6	3	6	2	0	1 0
The Giant Raft, 2 vols.:—							
I. 800 Leagues on the Amazon	7	6	3	6	2	0	1 0
II. The Cryptogram	7	6	3	6	2	0	1 0
The Green Ray	6	0	5	0	—		1 0
Godfrey Morgan	7	6	3	6	2	0	1 0
Kéraban the Inflexible:—							
I. Captain of the "Guidara"	7	6	3	6	2	0	1 0
II. Scarpante the Spy	7	6	3	6	2	0	1 0
The Archipelago on Fire	7	6	3	6	2	0	1 0
The Vanished Diamond	7	6	3	6	2	0	1 0
Mathias Sandorf	10	6	5	0	3	6	2 vols., 1s. each.
The Lottery Ticket	7	6	3	6			
The Clipper of the Clouds	7	6	3	6			
North against South	7	6					
Adrift in the Pacific	7	6					
Flight to France	7	6					

CELEBRATED TRAVELS AND TRAVELLERS. 3 vols. 8vo, 600 pp., 100 full-page illustrations, 12s. 6d. gilt edges, 14s. each:—(1) THE EXPLORATION OF THE WORLD. (2) THE GREAT NAVIGATORS OF THE EIGHTEENTH CENTURY. (3) THE GREAT EXPLORERS OF THE NINETEENTH CENTURY.

WALFORD (Mrs. L. B.) Her Great Idea, and other Stories.
Cr. 8vo, 10s. 6d.; also new ed., 6s.

Wallace (L.) Ben Hur: A Tale of the Christ. New Edition,
crown 8vo, 6s.; cheaper edition, 2s.

Wallack (L.) Memories of 50 Years; with many Portraits, and
Facsimiles. Small 4to, 63s. nett; ordinary edition 7s. 6d.

Waller (Rev. C.H.) Adoption and the Covenant. On Confirma-
tion. 2s. 6d.

—————— *Silver Sockets; and other Shadows of Redemption.*
Sermons at Christ Church, Hampstead. Small post 8vo, 6s.

—————— *The Names on the Gates of Pearl, and other Studies.*
New Edition. Crown 8vo, cloth extra, 3s. 6d.

—————— *Words in the Greek Testament.* Part I. Grammar.
Small post 8vo, cloth, 2s. 6d. Part II. Vocabulary, 2s. 6d.

Walsh (A. S.) Mary, Queen of the House of David. 8vo, 3s. 6d.

Walton (Iz.) Wallet Book, CIƆIƆLXXXV. Crown 8vo, half
vellum, 21s.; large paper, 42s.

—————— *Compleat Angler.* Lea and Dove Edition. Ed. by R. B.
MARSTON. With full-page Photogravures on India paper, and the
Woodcuts on India paper from blocks. 4to, half-morocco, 105s.;
large paper, royal 4to, full dark green morocco, gilt top, 210s.

Walton (T. H.) Coal Mining. With Illustrations. 4to, 25s.

War Scare in Europe. Crown 8vo, 2s. 6d.

Warner (C. D.) My Summer in a Garden. Boards, 1s.;
leatherette, 1s. 6d.; cloth, 2s.

—————— *Their Pilgrimage.* Illustrated by C. S. REINHART.
8vo, 7s. 6d.

Warren (W. F.) Paradise Found; the North Pole the Cradle
of the Human Race. Illustrated. Crown 8vo, 12s. 6d.

Washington Irving's Little Britain. Square crown 8vo, 6s.

Watson (P. B.) Swedish Revolution under Gustavus Vasa. 8vo.

Wells (H. P.) American Salmon Fisherman. 6s.

—————— *Fly Rods and Fly Tackle.* Illustrated. 10s. 6d.

Wells (J. W.) Three Thousand Miles through Brazil. Illustrated from Original Sketches. 2 vols. 8vo, 32s.

Wenzel (O.) Directory of Chemical Products of the German
Empire. 8vo, 25s.

Westgarth (W.) Half-century of Australasian Progress. Personal
retrospect. 8vo, 12s.

Wheatley (H. B.) Remarkable Bindings in the British Museum.
Reproductions in Colour, 94s. 6d., 73s. 6d., and 63s.

White (J.) Ancient History of the Maori; Mythology, &c.
Vols. I.-IV. 8vo, 10s. 6d. each.

White (R. Grant) England Without and Within. Crown 8vo,
10s. 6d.

—————— *Every-day English.* 10s. 6d.

White (R. Grant) Fate of Mansfield Humphreys, &c.   Cr. 8vo, 6s.
——— *Studies in Shakespeare.*   10s. 6d.
——— *Words and their Uses.*   New Edit., crown 8vo, 5s.
Whitney (Mrs.) The Other Girls.   A Sequel to "We Girls."
New ed.   12mo, 2s.
——— *We Girls.*   New Edition.   2s.
Whittier (J. G.) The King's Missive, and later Poems.   18mo,
choice parchment cover, 3s. 6d.
——— *St. Gregory's Guest, &c.*   Recent Poems.   5s.
William I. and the German Empire.   By G. BARNETT SMITH.
New Edition, 3s. 6d.
Willis-Bund (J.) Salmon Problems.   3s. 6d.; boards, 2s. 6d.
Wills (Dr. C. J.) Persia as it is.   Crown 8vo, 8s. 6d.
Wills, A Few Hints on Proving, without Professional Assistance.
By a PROBATE COURT OFFICIAL.   8th Edition, revised, with Forms
of Wills, Residuary Accounts, &c.   Fcap. 8vo, cloth limp, 1s.
Wilmot (A.) Poetry of South Africa Collected.   8vo, 6s.
Wilmot-Buxton (Ethel M.) Wee Folk, Good Folk: a Fantasy.
Illust., fcap. 4to, 5s.
Winder (Frederick Horatio) Lost in Africa: a Yarn of Adven-
ture.   Illust., cr. 8vo, 6s.
Winsor (Justin) Narrative and Critical History of America.
8 vols., 30s. each; large paper, per vol., 63s.
Woolsey.   Introduction to International Law.   5th Ed., 18s.
Woolson (Constance F.)   See "Low's Standard Novels."
Wright (H.) Friendship of God.   Portrait, &c.   Crown 8vo, 6s.
Wright (T.) Town of Cowper, Olney, &c.   6s.
Wrigley (M.) Algiers Illustrated.   100 Views in Photogravure.
Royal 4to, 45s.
Written to Order; the Journeyings of an Irresponsible Egotist.
By the Author of "A Day of my Life at Eton."   Crown 8vo, 6s.

YRIARTE (Charles) Florence: its History.   Translated by
C. B. PITMAN.   Illustrated with 500 Engravings.   Large imperial
4to, extra binding, gilt edges, 63s.; or 12 Parts, 5s. each.

ZILLMAN (J. H. L.) Past and Present Australian Life.
With Stories.   Crown 8vo, 2s.

London:

SAMPSON LOW, MARSTON, SEARLE, & RIVINGTON, LD.,
St. Dunstan's House,
FETTER LANE, FLEET STREET, E.C.

Gilbert and Rivington, Ld., St. John's House, Clerkenwell Road, E.C.